LET IT SNOW

A SAPPHIC CHRISTMAS ROMANCE

EMILY HAYES

1

Amanda scrolled down her computer screen, checking the numbers. She knew that she'd gotten them right the first time, but she always checked. The first step of running a successful business was ensuring that she knew where all of her money went.

Once she was satisfied that her accounts were all balanced, she opened photoshop and checked all of her current projects. Her greeting cards were looking spectacular, if she did say so herself.

It was a new venture Amanda was on. Her Christmas tree farm was doing well, but that only kept her busy around the holiday season. She made enough money there to carry her through the rest of the year, but Amanda wouldn't want to do nothing for eleven out of twelve months. She was always looking forward to her latest business idea.

Before she'd started the greeting cards, Amanda had made friendship bracelets and necklaces, but she hadn't done those in months. It reminded her too much of Nicole.

Amanda grimaced as she found herself once again thinking of her ex-wife. She and Nicole had made the bracelets and necklaces together, and after Nicole left her, Amanda hadn't been able to bring herself to keep the line going.

She had given over the rights entirely to Nicole. Amanda had been hurting too much to negotiate a good deal on the matter, so she had simply given that part of her business away. It wasn't like she needed the money anyway.

Amanda closed photoshop, deciding that she needed a distraction. She opened Tinder and started scrolling through potential matches. So far, Tinder had been a frustrating experience. It wasn't that there was a lack of attractive women there, but in the short interactions Amanda had had with a few of them, none of them had truly caught her interest.

It was six months since Nicole had left, and Amanda was ready to move on, but she was struggling to find someone who really thrilled her. Amanda knew that she deserved to be in a happy relationship with someone she found delightful. She was willing to wait for that to happen, but she couldn't help but feel discouraged.

She knew she was torturing herself for nothing, but Amanda couldn't help opening up Facebook and checking out Nicole's business page. They weren't friends on Facebook anymore, as things had ended rather badly between them, but Amanda still had access to Nicole's public pages.

She scrolled through the pictures and reviews. It looked like Nicole was doing well. Despite how badly things had ended between them, Amanda still wished Nicole the best. She was glad that Nicole seemed to be doing well, though it hurt her a little to see how quickly Nicole seemed to have moved on, taking the business' range even further than the two of them had when they had been working on it together.

Amanda forced herself to close Facebook and Tinder and open up photoshop again. Her greeting cards were doing so well that she had decided to do a special Christmas edition. Even though it was only mid-October, it was never too early to get started.

Most people were focusing on Halloween, but Amanda knew that Christmas was a far more lucrative holiday for greeting cards, so she was playing the long game rather than trying to rush things to make a few quick bucks off Halloween.

She started designing mock-ups of a couple of cards. She had her Christmas tree farm, and she had recently purchased a machine that would make fake snow. She planned to take multiple shots of both individual trees and groups of trees to use on her greeting cards, all covered in a fine layer of snow.

For some of the shots, she'd bring a Christmas tree inside under warm lighting and stack presents underneath. Amanda designed four cards before she decided she needed to take a break. She'd been at her computer for hours and the screen was starting to give her a headache.

She closed down photoshop and strolled out the back of her house, directly onto the farm part of her property. The trees ready for this season looked to be thriving. There was an automated sprinkler system, so Amanda didn't need to worry about watering them, but she still needed to keep an eye on them. If any of them started to look bedraggled or diseased, she would have to cut down the defective tree so that it didn't negatively impact the other trees.

The trees were all looking good. Amanda sank down to the ground with her back against one of the larger trees, sighing in satisfaction. When things became too much, a walk through her trees always made her feel better.

She closed her eyes and focused on the gentle breeze playing over her face.

She was pulled from her reverie by her phone ringing. Amanda answered it automatically without checking the caller ID. She was a businesswoman and had to answer her phone, as she never knew when it could be a potential customer.

She regretted not checking the ID the moment she heard the voice on the other end. "Hello, Amanda."

Amanda grimaced. "Nicole."

"I wanted to give you an update on our bracelet and necklace range. It's doing really well, and I'm thinking of creating a category of spooky Halloween-themed bracelets."

"That's great, Nicole, but what does this have to do with me?"

"Well, since business is booming, I thought it would only be fair to share the profits."

Amanda ground her teeth, a horrible habit that her dentist had reprimanded her for more than once. "I already told you. I signed over the rights to those bracelets to you. I don't want anything more to do with them." *Or to do with you.* But she didn't say that.

"Don't be ridiculous, Amanda," Nicole snapped. "You're supposed to be a good businesswoman, for God's sake! You don't just turn down free royalties. That's a stupid move."

"I raised my business from the ground up! I don't need to hear it from you about business decisions, not when you got your start-up money from daddy's trust!"

Amanda knew her words were a mistake from the moment they left her lips.

"At least I'm *trying* to be civil about this! I left you, Amanda, but you're acting like I killed your cat! What the hell is wrong with you?"

What was wrong was that after years and years of endless fights, Amanda had had enough. Nicole wasn't a bad person, but they both had such strong personalities, it was no wonder they fought all the time.

Amanda had been devastated when Nicole left her, and it still hurt sometimes, but over the past few months, she had come to realize that it had been the best decision for both of them.

Amanda forced herself to take several deep breaths. "I don't need the money, Nicole, least of all from you. For the last time, I signed those rights over to you. I don't want to hear from you again. If I need to tell you again, it'll be coming from my lawyer."

She hung up the phone, breathing hard. Nicole didn't call back. Smart of her. Amanda wasn't kidding about the lawyer. All she wanted was to put that horrible chapter of her life behind her.

Of course, it hadn't been all bad. She had loved Nicole once, and they had had many good times together before it became apparent that their personalities simply weren't a match for a long-term relationship. They had hung on for six years, but everyone had their breaking points.

Well, there went the serenity she had gained by

walking through her trees. Amanda clambered to her feet and started walking again, a little faster than before. The trees flashed by almost too fast for her to get a good evaluation of how they were growing, but she didn't slow.

She tried to quiet her mind and distracted herself by thinking about the greeting cards she was working on.

Amanda's legs were aching by the time her mind was quiet, but it was worth it. She limped back to the house and flopped onto the couch. She went back onto her phone, flicking through Tinder. She truly wanted to meet someone she could fall in love with again, not to mention have sex with.

God, Amanda missed sex. She hadn't been with anyone since Nicole, and she was feeling the lack of sex, for sure. Whatever else could be said about their relationship, the sex with Nicole was excellent. That was part of what had kept them together for so long.

Masturbation was great, but it just wasn't the same. Amanda had even considered hiring an escort for an evening or two, but in the end, she had decided that she didn't want to have meaningless sex. She wanted it to be with someone she cared for, or was at least interested in.

Amanda lay back, fantasizing about finding someone she could spoil and adore. Someone who didn't find issue with everything she said and turn every action into an argument. She wanted someone peaceful and calm—two things that Nicole never was.

No one on Tinder seemed to fit the bill, either. Amanda supposed that she simply had to keep trying. Finding the right person was hard work, just like running a business.

Thoughts of running a business brought her back to Nicole. Amanda truly hoped that she didn't need to get lawyers involved in this, but she would if she had to. She needed peace, and Nicole was the least peaceful person Amanda had ever encountered. Passionate, absolutely, but peaceful? Not a chance.

She gave up on Tinder for now and went back to her computer. For a couple more hours, Amanda lost herself in designing greeting cards. She loved this part of her work, and often spent so long at the computer that she lost track of time and only realized when her shoulders started aching that she'd been at it for most of the day.

One thing was certain, Amanda was going to make sure that her greeting cards were the talk of the season this Christmas.

2

Snow finished up with Bluebell's school lunch before walking with her to the bus stop.

"Have a good day at school, honey."

"I will, Mom! Our science teacher says we'll be doing volcanoes today."

Snow smiled fondly at her daughter. "That sounds wonderful."

Bluebell loved everything to do with volcanoes. Snow hoped to take her to see a real volcano someday (an inactive one, of course), if she could afford to take the trip.

Snow returned home, where her mom was painting. Snow stood behind her for a few minutes to watch. She always loved seeing Daisy paint. She was so talented, and her paintings earned them a mostly steady income.

Daisy turned to look at her. "You're being creepy again." She smiled warmly at Snow, showing that she didn't truly mind.

"I can't help it. It's so mesmerizing watching you paint. I wish you'd let me take photos of you like this."

"This time when I'm painting needs to be my time

alone. I don't mind sharing my work with the world, but only when I'm good and ready."

"I know, but a girl can dream."

Daisy winked at her. "You always were a dreamer. You take after me that way."

Snow watched for a few more minutes before going to her bedroom and grabbing her camera. It was the perfect day for photos—slightly overcast, which cut out the direct glare of the sun, but not so dark that it appeared gloomy.

She walked to the park with her camera gear strapped to her back. Snow could have driven, but she loved being outdoors and didn't mind the walk.

When she got to the park, she started lining up shots. She did one of a tall, gnarled tree that looked like it had been there for hundreds of years. She found a small pine that would make the perfect Christmas tree shot.

Snow was particularly pleased with that one. She had a small range of greeting cards that she created using her own photos and wanted to do a special Christmas line. She'd kill to get some photos of real Christmas trees, especially with families around them, but she couldn't afford to hire models or to rent space on a tree farm.

Still, she would make do. When the first snows of the season started, that would make for a lot of magical photos. Snow would come back to this pine and do a few more photos. Maybe she could have her mother and Bluebell in a few of them to add a family tone to the cards.

Next, she photographed a bush with bright orange berries, followed by a perfect red-orange oak leaf that had fallen to the ground. Snow's eyes were drawn to the playground. That would make a perfect photo, but she didn't take photos of people without their permission. Most people didn't want to be photographed by some stranger, especially since those photos would be going on publicly available gift cards.

Snow spent a total of three hours in the park before heading back home. She got a few good photo opportunities on the way back, too. The clouds shifted just a little to allow a ray of sunlight through to the ground. Snow got a good shot of that ray, already planning how she was going to incorporate it into her greeting cards.

When she got home, she sat down at her computer and opened photoshop. She had several new gift cards in the making. This was always her favorite part—designing the gift cards. Getting them printed and selling them was important, but she didn't particularly enjoy the business aspect of her job.

Photography was her passion, but Snow needed to earn an income, so she did what she had to by getting her cards printed out on high-quality paper and managing a Facebook page where she did her best to promote her products.

She was immersed in designing the card with that beautiful ray of sunlight when her phone rang. Snow answered it immediately out of habit. She got a lot of people calling to ask about her greeting cards and didn't want to miss a potential customer.

She was also part of a freelance agency that interfaced with clients and assigned photographers to clients for once-off jobs. This could be a client calling who had gotten her number from the agency. Snow hoped so. She always loved finding out what ideas other people had and bringing them to life.

"Hello?"

"Hello, is this Snow Willows?"

"Yes, it is. How may I help you?"

"This is Jake Mason from the National Photography Foundation. We're pleased to tell you that you've won our grand prize for the best nature photograph of the year."

Snow's mouth popped open. Her mom had encouraged her to enter that contest, but she never dreamed in a million years that she might actually win.

"I—I won? You're sure you've got the right person?"

"Quite sure. Your photo of that sunrise was captured perfectly; all of the judges said so."

Snow couldn't believe it. She knew that she had a great eye when doing nature shots particularly, she could look at any scene and her mind would easily pick out the bits that would make the best photographs, but she had never thought she was good enough to win such a prestigious award.

"I—thank you. Thank you so much."

"We'll need you to come down to headquarters to collect your trophy and cash prize."

Snow choked on saliva as she swallowed wrong. She'd forgotten all about the cash prize—the ten- thousand-dollar cash prize. She gasped for air, trying to at least sound like she had it together.

"I can do that. When is good for you?"

"We've got someone there during working hours, so whenever works for you."

"Thank you. I'll be there by one, then."

"Great. Oh, and there are some reporters who'd like to interview you about your photos. I'll let them know when to expect you."

Snow's face hurt from smiling. She'd never imagined, even in her wildest fantasies, that people would like her photos so much they wanted to interview her about them.

"I'll be happy to talk to the reporters."

"Excellent. Well, I'll see you soon, then. Goodbye, Snow."

Snow hung up with trembling fingers. Then she leapt up, punching the air and letting out a whoop of triumph.

"What are we whooping about?" Daisy wandered through with blue paint smudged on her nose.

"Mom, I won! I won the award from the National Photography Foundation!"

Daisy's face split into a wide grin. "I knew you could do it, Snow! That's fantastic!" She threw her arms around Snow and the two of them hugged fiercely.

"It's got a huge cash prize too." Snow's mind was already spinning ahead. With such a large cash prize, she could afford to buy her own high-quality printer. It would significantly reduce the running costs of her greeting card business, as she wouldn't need to pay for the printing company to print out all of her cards.

With the extra income she would earn from those lower expenses, she could afford to start a college fund for Bluebell. Snow was practically buzzing with excitement. She decided to buy Bluebell that ridiculously expensive doll she'd been asking for for weeks now after the interview. What was the point of winning a huge cash prize if you didn't splurge a little?

Snow spent about twenty minutes dressing carefully. If she was going to be interviewed, she wanted to look her best.

She chose an airy blue dress made out of thin fabric coming to little points on the sleeves and bottom hem. It was fancier than what she usually wore and brought out the bright shimmering blue of her eyes, and Snow was glad for an excuse to wear it. Fortunately, though the weather had been cooler recently, today was a warm enough day to wear a dress made out of such thin fabric.

Snow also did her makeup, something she seldom did except for very special occasions. Once she was done, she checked her phone for the time. She still had two hours before she had to walk Bluebell home from the bus stop.

Most kids walked home by themselves from the bus stop, but Snow used any chance to go for a walk outside and loved spending quality time with her daughter.

When she got to the National Photography Foundation's headquarters, there was a small crowd of people outside.

Snow tried to edge around them, but when they caught sight of her, they converged around her, surrounding her on all sides.

"Are you Snow Willows?"

"What was the inspiration for your sunrise picture?"

"Where do you see your career going from here?"

"Other than the one that won the competition, what do you think is your best picture to date?"

Snow didn't even have time to answer one question before another reporter was asking a different one. She had the urge to run; she didn't like small spaces, and the photographers were crowding her.

Snow forced herself to stand her ground. This was too good a career opportunity to miss. She could get so much visibility for her work if these interviews went well. She'd be crazy not to do her best.

"Please, one question at a time." Snow nodded at the reporter closest to her, who didn't hesitate.

"What made you choose that particular photo to send in for the contest?"

"Well, apart from it being one of my best photos, I

hoped that even if I didn't win the contest, it would bring a smile to the judges' faces. Sunrises are always so inspirational and hopeful. I guess I just wanted to spread some joy. Sunrise is my favorite time of day. The light at that time is just the most beautiful."

"How do you feel, knowing that you've won?"

"I'm still in shock, to be honest. I never imagined I'd win. But I'm delighted, of course. It just needs a little more time to sink in."

"What do you think this means for your career in photography?"

"I honestly don't know. I mean, I'm hoping my work will get more visibility. I have my own greeting cards business that I create from the photos I take, so hopefully more people will find out about that. I also take on freelance jobs sometimes, so perhaps I will get more of those."

"Would you say you deserve this prestigious award?"

That was a tough one. Snow honestly wasn't sure. She had never thought she would win, but she had, and that said something. "I don't think I'm qualified to judge that, but the judges of this competition have chosen me for the award, and I am most honored by their decision."

She stood outside for almost an hour, answering different questions. Snow gave out the link to her Facebook page with her greeting cards, as well as her email address and the email address of her freelance agency for anyone wanting a photography job done.

Finally, Snow had to put a halt to the questions that never seemed to end. "I need to get going now. I need to pick my daughter up from school soon."

Of course, that brought up a whole new flurry of questions, which Snow politely declined. "You have my email address. If anyone has any further questions, I'll be happy to arrange follow-up interviews. For now, I have to go."

She hurried into the building and closed the door behind her. Snow took a deep, calming breath. That had been intense, but not in a bad way. She was sure that her work would get a lot more visibility in the coming weeks.

The actual picking up of the award was easy. They had it ready for her, and Snow simply gave them her banking details for the cash prize, which reflected just a few minutes after they did the transfer. The reporters were still hanging around outside, and Snow once more turned down their questions as courteously as she could.

She made it to the bus stop just in time, right as the bus was pulling up.

Bluebell bounced out of the bus, grinning broadly. "Mom! Mom, we did the volcano, and it even exploded!"

"Wow! Did the teacher let you help?"

"He did! I poured the stuff into the volcano to make it explode."

Snow was glad to hear it. "That's wonderful, honey."

She took Bluebell's hand and started leading her down the street.

"Mom, home is that way."

"I know, but we're not going home just yet. I thought we could go to the toy store. I've decided to get you that doll you've been wanting."

Bluebell's eyes widened. "Really?"

"Yes, really."

Bluebell flung her arms around Snow. "You're the best, Mom!"

Snow chuckled, hugging Bluebell back before turning to continue the short walk to the toy store.

They left the toy store about twenty minutes later with

a very happy Bluebell, already talking animatedly to her new doll.

When they got home, Daisy was waiting for them and ushered Snow into the lounge. "Look!"

Snow stared in astonishment. She was on TV, talking to reporters outside the Foundation building. She was pleased to see that she didn't look nearly as flustered as she had felt answering all of those questions.

Daisy put an arm around Snow. "I'm so proud of you, honey."

"Thanks, Mom."

"Mom, why are you on TV?"

"It's because I won an award, sweetheart, for one of the photos I took. The reporters were asking me questions about my photos."

"That's so cool!"

"It is indeed very cool," Snow agreed. "Now, shall we look at your homework?"

Bluebell nodded enthusiastically. "We need to answer questions about the volcano!"

"And do your math homework," Snow reminded her.

Bluebell wilted slightly. "And do my math homework." Bluebell hated math, something Snow privately agreed with her on, but she did her best to encourage her daughter and to make the homework as fun as possible for her.

Homework didn't go as planned. Snow's phone was practically blowing up with all the notifications she was getting. Eventually, she asked Daisy to help Bluebell with her homework so that she could focus on all the incoming notifications.

Most of them were from her Facebook page, ordering greeting cards. Snow's eyes went wide as she saw how many orders she was getting. She would need to get that printer tomorrow and start printing as soon as possible to fulfill all of these orders in a timely fashion.

There were a couple of emails asking her to do photo shoots, and a multitude of emails from reporters asking for interviews. Twitter was already calling her a *local sensation*.

It was all so incredible; Snow couldn't stop smiling. She checked the time and saw that if she drove, she still had time to go to the computer store today to get her printer. She generally preferred to walk, but walking home carrying a heavy printer wouldn't be fun anyway.

She told Daisy where she was going and got into the car that the two of them shared. Snow hummed as she drove. Today was the best day she could remember having in a while, and all indications were that the days to follow would be just as good.

3

It started off as an ordinary day. Amanda went for a walk through her trees, checking that they were all growing well. Then she went to her computer and looked through the greeting cards she had designed so far.

She was browsing through Facebook, checking if she had any questions on her page, when she saw a link to an article about some local photographer. Apparently, she'd won a national award. Amanda didn't know why this was turning up on her Facebook, but she opened the link anyway.

Amanda scanned the article, which said that the photographer, Snow Willows, also had her own range of greeting cards. Amanda navigated to Snow's Facebook page to find it flooded with questions about her greeting cards. By all appearances, people were going crazy over the things.

Amanda scowled as she looked through the selection of greeting cards. These were good—almost as good as Amanda's. A quick Google search told her that this Snow was quickly building a local following. Everyone was raving about her greeting cards and encouraging her to do a special Christmas line.

A little further reading told Amanda that Snow planned to do just that. She ground her teeth as she glared at the screen. This Snow Willows was stealing Amanda's thunder! It was Amanda's greeting cards that were supposed to capture the minds of the masses this Christmas season. How was that supposed to happen when all anyone wanted to talk about was Snow bloody Willows and how incredible her cards were?

Amanda hated her. She hated everything from her stupid talent to her idiotic pretty face and bright blue eyes to her annoyingly well-shaped ass, which was clearly visible as she walked away from reporters.

She couldn't be very intelligent, either. Who walked away from reporters? She should have stayed and answered questions as long as there were reporters to ask them. Clearly, this Snow wasn't a very good businesswoman.

Well, Amanda wasn't going to give in that easily. She needed to find a way to make her greeting cards truly spectacular; she would outshine Snow.

Perhaps it was time to think of hiring a professional photographer. Amanda took decent photos, but she couldn't deny that the quality wasn't quite up to the standard of the photos that Snow used on her cards.

Amanda was willing to put as much money as she needed into this. It wasn't even about the business anymore. It was about beating Snow. No one would steal her thunder this Christmas and get away with it.

Amanda got onto Google and quickly found the top

freelance agency for photographers. She dialed their number and waited.

"Hello, how may I help you?"

"Hi. I need someone to take photos for me, tomorrow. And probably a number of days after that. Send me your best."

"Our best photographer is currently booked up until—"

"I'll double whatever their current engagements are paying. Just have them to me tomorrow."

"I—well, I suppose we could send another photographer on those jobs. Very well, you will have her tomorrow. What's your address?"

Amanda gave her address and hung up. She spent a few minutes on online banking making the deposit for the job before returning to her computer. She forced herself to exit everything that had anything to do with Snow. Her pretty face, her blonde hair, her perfect fucking cards. It was just making her angry.

Instead, she focused on making a list of all the potential shots she wanted *her* photographer to do. This was going to be great. Soon, everyone would see that no one outshone Amanda Asher.

THE NEXT DAY, Amanda's doorbell rang at exactly nine o'clock, the time she had arranged for the photographer to come.

She opened the door, smiling.

Her smile dropped off her face when she saw who it was. She recognized the woman immediately from the footage she had watched yesterday. Bright blue expectant eyes, lovely blonde hair, pretty heart shaped face.

It was Snow Willows.

Anger coiled in Amanda's gut. She knew the freelance agency hadn't done this on purpose, but having the very person she was trying to beat felt like a someone was spitting in her face.

She glared at Snow, whose friendly smile faltered.

4

S now smiled uncertainly at her new client, Amanda Asher. Amanda was glaring at her as though Snow had personally offended her. Snow didn't know what she could have possibly done to offend the woman already. Perhaps she was misreading her expression.

"Hi, I'm Snow. I'm here to take photos for you." She stuck out her hand, but Amanda didn't take it.

She gave Snow another forbidding glower before turning away. "Come," she called over her shoulder.

Snow was a little miffed. There was no need for Amanda to be so cold and rude. After all, Snow was here on short notice. The company had cancelled her previous engagement to make sure she could be here for Amanda today. Had Snow had her way, she wouldn't let a client down, even for one who was paying more, but the agency thought otherwise.

Snow forgot her annoyance as she walked through Amanda's house and out the back to a field full of beautiful Christmas trees.

"Oh," Snow breathed softly. "This is wonderful. Is this what you want me to take photos of? Your trees?"

"No, I just want you to gape at them like an idiot," Amanda snapped. "Of course, I want you to take photos!"

Snow bit back a retort. Amanda was a client, after all, and the agency wouldn't be very happy with her if she did anything to make Amanda angrier than she already was.

Snow got out her equipment and started setting up.

"Wait. Don't do that yet. I haven't finished setting the scene."

Snow sat back on her heels while Amanda filled in snow with a loud, noisy machine. She didn't see why she couldn't set up while Amanda did that. Amanda seemed overly bossy and rude.

Why, then, did Snow find her attractive? Amanda Asher was tall and classically beautiful with high cheekbones and eyes that were full of intensity and depth. Snow struggled to place Amanda's age, she didn't look that much older than Snow's own thirty five years, but Snow noticed the fine lines in the corners of her eyes and the hint of grey hair at her temples and thought perhaps Amanda was about fifty. And still, so very beautiful.

God, I'd love to photograph her. Her face is mesmerising. If only she wasn't such an ass!

"Well, what are you waiting for? Set up your camera! These photos aren't going to take themselves, you know."

Snow resisted the urge to roll her eyes. She should be thinking resentful thoughts about Amanda right now, not wondering what it would feel like to have Amanda order her to strip down. She definitely shouldn't be imagining Amanda pinning her to one of those Christmas trees and thoroughly ravishing her.

Snow felt herself blushing as she set up her equipment. She needed to focus on the job at hand and save her naughty fantasies for later. Amanda tapped her foot as Snow worked, looking determinedly away from her.

Snow didn't know why Amanda seemed to have such an instant problem with her, but at least Amanda wouldn't see her blushing if she didn't even look at her.

Snow started snapping shots of the trees. The fake snow made them look so beautiful. Snow loved nothing more than capturing pure beauty. If she could afford it, she would even have offered to do this photoshoot for free. Taking these pictures was a reward in and of itself.

She glanced at Amanda out of the corner of her eye. Amanda was wearing a thick red jacket that hugged her curves and dark brown pants. The outfit was perfect on her, making her look both distinguished and sexy at the same time.

Snow looked again at the trees she was photographing. Amanda would look amazing in these photos. Snow wondered if she could convince Amanda of that.

"Take some of individual trees, too. No, not that one! That one is limp, can't you see? This one is much better. Yes, that's right. These are for greeting cards and I want some with just one tree, so make sure you don't get any of the others in the background."

"I'm also selling greeting cards this season," Snow said brightly, trying to make conversation.

Amanda gave her a withering look. "How lovely," she practically snarled.

Snow couldn't help backing up a step at the venom in Amanda's eyes. What was wrong with this woman? Good thing she was so striking to look at, because her stellar personality certainly wasn't going to win her any dates.

Snow took a few more pictures before deciding to put her idea to Amanda.

"I was thinking... maybe you could be in some of the photos."

"What? No, that's not what I brought you here for. This isn't a vanity shoot. These are for my greeting cards."

"I really think it will add to them, honestly. It would give the cards a more personal feel. You have exactly the right look."

Amanda hesitated, her fierce expression faltering. "I don't know..."

"Just let me try? Please? If you don't like the shots, you can delete them afterward."

"I... alright, but just a few photos. Then get back to what I hired you for."

"Of course." Snow beamed as she gestured for Amanda to move into the line of her lens. "If you stand there and clasp your hands in front of you. Perfect. Now tilt your head just a bit to the—yes, that's right. Can you let your hair down?"

Amanda pulled the hair tie out of her long brunette hair and shook it out. Her hair was just as lovely as Snow had imagined it might be for the photos, long and wavy and shiny and not too perfectly 'done.'

It was clear that Amanda was no novice when it came to lining up a good shot. She positioned herself perfectly and Snow snapped picture after picture.

God, she's a natural. Her face just looks so striking in the light. Those high cheekbones, those full lips, those lovely dark green eyes that match the green of the Christmas trees exactly.

"Now maybe you can sit in front of the tree? There, perfect."

Snow took a few more shots before hesitantly coming

forward. "I want to put a bit of the snow on you, to make it look like you've been sitting outside for a while. Is that okay?"

"Fine, just get on with it."

Snow started scooping the fake snow up and gently patting it onto Amanda's jacket. Amanda looked up at her with an intense gaze, her anger seemingly abated for now. They were very close together, and Snow slowly brought her hand to Amanda's arm, rubbing a bit of fake snow off the coat and repositioning it.

Amanda watched her with her full lips slightly parted. Snow wondered what it would be like to kiss those lips. She couldn't help leaning a little closer to Amanda than she needed to when reaching down for the next handful of snow.

Their faces were inches apart now. Snow was almost certain that Amanda was going to lean forward and kiss her, but at the last moment, Amanda turned away.

"That should be enough," Snow said softly. She got up and walked shakily to her camera. That had been intense, even though she and Amanda had barely touched. She took several deep breaths before getting behind her camera and taking some shots.

"Could you tilt you head a little to the right, please, Amanda?"

Amanda did as she was asked without argument. Snow could see her patience wearing thin and got shots from as many different angles as she could.

"That's enough of this. I want you to take more shots of the trees."

Snow dipped her head. "Of course, Amanda."

A flash of red caught her eye, almost as bright as Amanda's jacket. "Can I pick some of these berries from the bushes? I think they would look wonderful in this tree here. I can get some close up shots of the branches with the berries in them."

"Fine, do what you want. Just get me some decent photos."

Snow gathered the berries and got the shots she wanted. She felt inspired by her beautiful surroundings, and the beauty of Amanda's face. It was such a buzz to work with a beautiful model who wasn't her mom or Bluebell. Amanda may not be pleasant company, but she was more stunning than all the Christmas trees, snow and berries in the world.

"What kind of name is Snow, anyway?"

Snow smiled. As a child, she had been teased a lot for her name, but she didn't let it bother her now. "I was born during a week of heavy snow. My mother thought that it was the fates telling her what to name me."

"Hippie nonsense," Amanda muttered.

Snow didn't respond, which seemed to irritate Amanda, who appeared to be gunning for some kind of confrontation. Too bad for her that Snow wasn't a confrontational person. She let insults and bad attitudes slide off her. She didn't have time for that kind of negative energy.

"Alright, I think I'm done here, unless you want photos of anything else?"

"No, there's nothing else. Off you go, then."

Snow supposed that a thank you was too much to hope for. "Thank you for your business, Amanda. I will edit those photos tonight and get them to you tomorrow morning."

Amanda seemed briefly surprised. "That fast?"

"It usually takes longer," Snow admitted. "I'm excited

about these shots, though. I want to get working on them as soon as possible, and once I start working, I tend to get drawn in. I may be up the whole night doing it, but it'll be a night well spent. You'll have them tomorrow morning."

"Excellent. I do enjoy efficiency."

"Goodbye, Amanda."

Amanda waved her imperiously out of the door.

As Snow made her way home, she couldn't get Amanda out of her mind. She wondered if Amanda would like some more photos taken. Snow would be more than happy to get another chance to photograph Amanda.

She groaned as she realized that she had developed something of a crush on Amanda, despite the fact that Amanda Asher was a total ass. She was just so *beautiful* and Snow had such a thing for beauty in every form, and Amanda's bossy attitude was strangely alluring.

Snow was grinning widely as she stepped inside. She went straight to her computer and started working on the photos. Snow gasped as she opened up the folder.

These were spectacular. She thought that they must be the best photos she had ever taken—even better than the one that had won her that award.

She had just been so inspired by Amanda and her Christmas trees; it had taken her photography skills to a whole different level. Snow resolved to thank Amanda for the opportunity if she ever had occasion to see her again.

She imagined running into Amanda in the grocery store, or out in the park. It was unlikely, of course. Amanda lived in a much better area than Snow and would likely not shop or walk in the same places as her.

Snow grinned as she kept working on the photos, paying particular attention to the ones with Amanda in them. She wanted to be sure Amanda loved the photos.

Maybe she would request Snow again. Snow hoped she would. She already had ideas for some other shots they could take.

She dove headfirst into the work and didn't emerge until hours later when her stomach was growling and it was nearly time to pick Bluebell up from school. Snow couldn't stop grinning the whole way to the bus stop.

5

Amanda didn't expect Snow to send the photos through the next day, even though she had said she would. Though Snow had been nothing but courteous and professional, Amanda still hated her. Snow might seem sweet and innocent, but she had stolen Amanda's glory with her Christmas cards, and that wasn't something Amanda could easily forgive.

Amanda knew that she was possibly overreacting, but she couldn't help it. She had been so excited about her cards being the talk of the season, and Snow had taken that from her, even though it hadn't been intentional.

Well, wouldn't it just be the perfect karmic justice if the photos Snow took helped Amanda's cards out-sell Snow's own cards? If she was as good as the agency said she was, Amanda would have a good chance once she got those photos.

Her email pinged and she checked it, surprised to see that Snow had sent the photos already. Amanda opened the first one and gaped at it.

It was a picture of her, covered in snow, sitting in front

of a Christmas tree. Amanda knew that she was an attractive woman, but this photo didn't just make her look attractive—it made her look ethereal and like a model.

She flicked to the next one, which was just as good as the first, a shot of her standing in front of one of the trees. It had been taken when she didn't realize she was being photographed. Amanda felt her jaw dropping even further as she looked through the rest of the photos.

Snow wasn't just good. She was *brilliant*.

Amanda's jaw snapped shut. Of course, Snow had to be brilliant. She was the talk of the town, a local celebrity. She was sweet and kind, and she had talent that Amanda could only dream of.

Amanda hated her for it.

She looked through the photos again, trying to find something she could complain about, but there was absolutely nothing. They were perfect.

She kept coming back to the pictures of herself. Amanda had never seen herself look this good—in the mirror or in any photo. She wanted to make one of the photos her Facebook profile picture, but that felt like it would be letting Snow win.

Snow would no doubt see the picture and be pleased that Amanda liked it. Amanda didn't want Snow to know she liked the pictures, but she supposed that couldn't be helped. Snow would see that they were on Amanda's greeting cards, after all.

Amanda changed her Facebook profile to the first picture Snow had sent, the one with her covered in fake snow, and posted a couple of the others of the trees on her website, the ones that she didn't plan to use for greeting cards. They were stunning and would make for great advertising.

She didn't credit Snow in any of the captions. Amanda knew that she was supposed to—that was the agreement she had made with the agency, after all—but she wasn't going to give Snow the satisfaction of having her name spread even further by Amanda's business.

Almost immediately, Amanda started getting likes and comments on her Facebook photo. A couple of people asked her who took the shot, but Amanda didn't give names. She just told them that a photographer from the agency came over to take them. She wasn't going to credit Snow.

Let Snow see what it feels like to have what is owed to you taken away by someone else. Amanda should have had this season of greeting cards unopposed. It's only fair that Snow was punished by not receiving credit that she deserved.

Amanda checked her watch and saw that the time had sped by while she had been looking at the photos. She needed to hurry or she was going to be late for lunch with Emily.

Emily and Amanda had been best friends since college and saw each other for lunch once a week. When Amanda rushed into the café, Emily was already there waiting for her.

"Hey, Amanda." Emily smiled as Amanda sat down. "I love your new photos! You look stunning, particularly in the one you made your Facebook profile picture."

Amanda practically glowed under the praise. "Thank you. I am very pleased with them. Did you see the ones I put on my website?"

"I did! Those ones with the berries are inspired. Did you take them?"

The berries had been Snow's idea, Amanda remembered sourly. "No, I hired a photographer."

Just the thought of Snow made her grit her teeth in annoyance.

"Amanda? Are you okay?"

"I just—it's this photographer. Her name is Snow. Who is called Snow, anyway? What kind of stupid name is that?"

Emily opened her mouth to reply, but Amanda was on a roll now and kept talking.

"She went and stole my audience for my greeting cards, and then she has the nerve to walk into my house and start taking photos like I need her!"

"She just came to your house and randomly asked to take photos?"

"No," Amanda admitted. "I called a photography agency and asked them to send their best photographer. They sent Snow."

"So, you hired her. And you got angry when she showed up as you requested?"

"Well, it sounds stupid when you say it like that."

"Is there something to the story that I'm missing?"

"Yeah, there is. She stole from me."

"She stole something? Did you report her to the police?"

"She didn't steal something I could report her for. My greeting cards were supposed to take everyone by storm this season, but that can't happen when everyone is cooing over *Snow bloody Willows*." Amanda spat out her name.

"You're jealous, then. You're jealous of her talent and success, and you took it out on her, when she was only doing her job."

"You're making me sound unreasonable."

"That's because you're acting unreasonable, Amanda. The poor woman isn't launching a personal attack on you. She's just trying to run her business, the same as you are. I hope you weren't rude to her."

"I..." Amanda knew that she had been rude to Snow. Was Emily right? Was she being completely irrational?

It didn't take long to come up with that answer. Yes, of course she was being irrational. Anger and resentment weren't always rational emotions, though.

"So I might have been a bit snappish," Amanda admitted. "So what? She's a professional. She can take cranky customers."

"She can, but she shouldn't have to. You can be a real ass when you want to be, you know? You're letting your quick temper get ahead of you. I know that things are bad between you and Nicole, but you can't take that out on other people who happen to annoy you."

"Who said this has anything to do with Nicole?"

"Doesn't it?"

"No!"

"So, you didn't have an upsetting interaction with Nicole just before you went on this vendetta against Snow?"

"Have you been listening in on my phone calls?"

Emily chuckled. "No, I just know you. When you're hurting, you tend to lash out. And I call you out on your bullshit. It's why you need me."

"That I do," Amanda sighed. "Maybe I am being unfair to Snow, but I can't help how I feel. I know it's not rational, but that doesn't make it go away."

"Well, it's not like you're going to see her again. I'm

sure the anger will fade on its own eventually. Just don't treat her badly if you do happen to run into her."

Amanda could try, but just the thought of stupid lovely Snow with her stupid name and her stupid talent put her on edge. Her pretty warm smile and her brilliant blue eyes. It was all too much. She didn't know if she could manage to be civil with the woman. But that shouldn't be a problem. She had her photos. She didn't need anything else from Snow.

Unbidden, the memory Amanda had been trying very hard to ignore popped up.

She remembered how close she and Snow had been when Snow was getting her ready for that photo. Snow had looked so beautiful in the light with her golden hair and the trees in the background.

Snow was at least fifteen years younger than her, and probably wouldn't be interested in someone as old as Amanda, who had had her fifty-second birthday just last week.

That didn't stop Amanda from finding her attractive. She had that sweet, innocent, free-spirited look about her. She was so different from Nicole, who was argumentative, controlling and down-to-business, just like Amanda.

In that moment, Amanda hadn't been angry with Snow. She had simply been taken by her beauty. She wondered what it would be like to kiss Snow's pillowy pink lips. She nearly had, in that moment, but had pulled back just in time.

Of course, Snow wouldn't want that, especially after how Amanda had treated her. So, Amanda pushed that memory to the back of her mind and focused instead on how much she hated Snow and her stupidly beautiful lips.

"Amanda? Are you still with me?"

"What?"

"You zoned out for a moment. I hope you're not planning on doing something to get vengeance on poor Snow?"

Not unless kissing her pretty pink lips and then fucking her senseless against a Christmas tree counted as vengeance. No. She wasn't thinking of that right now.

"No, I'm not planning anything like that. I want to get working on those greeting cards. The photos are wonderful, and I think they will sell really well."

"Agreed! I'll leave you to it, then. Same time next week?"

"Same time next week. See you, Emily."

"Bye, Amanda."

Amanda did her best not to think of Snow on the drive home and mostly succeeded. She sat down at her computer and started designing her greeting cards with the new photos.

After about ten minutes, she realized that she had stopped and was simply staring at the photos, remarking internally over how beautiful they were.

Amanda looked again at the photo of her in the snow by the trees. She went to her Tinder profile and updated it as her profile photo. Maybe she'd have more luck with a more attractive photo of her as her profile.

Things without Nicole were calmer and better in many ways, but Amanda was lonely. She had her business, and that was enough to sustain her, but she wanted more.

She suddenly thought again of Snow and wondered if she was on Tinder. Amanda shut down that thought at once. There were plenty of women around, women who didn't set her teeth on edge just by their mere existence.

She scrolled through Tinder for a few minutes, but didn't find any likely matches, not that that was a surprise. Amanda was very picky when it came to potential partners.

She closed down Tinder and focused once more on her greeting cards. She was already getting positive feedback on her website about the photos of her trees. Amanda received a couple of email enquiries about purchasing trees, which she answered before returning to designing the cards.

Thoughts of Nicole and Snow faded as she focused on making the best greeting cards she could. She would outshine Snow with her spectacular cards. Amanda would see to it.

6

S now knew that this was probably a bad idea, but she was here now, so she may as well stay.

She had driven several areas over to do her grocery shopping in the mall nearest Amanda's house. It was stupid, but she was hoping to see Amanda again.

Amanda hadn't responded to Snow's email, but Snow was sure she had seen the photos by now. She wasn't expecting Amanda to thank her, not after her awful attitude yesterday, but Snow still found herself wanting to see Amanda again, regardless of whether she would receive any gratitude.

So, here she was, buying ridiculously expensive groceries all in a pathetic attempt to spot the subject of her crush.

Snow looked around as she walked, but didn't spot Amanda anywhere. She was just about to give up when she saw a flash of red.

Amanda was wearing the same coat she had worn yesterday. She was just getting into her car, and Snow hurried to catch up to her.

"Amanda!"

Amanda was just closing her door and didn't appear to hear Snow. Snow sighed in defeat as Amanda drove away.

"Did you want to speak to Amanda?"

She turned to an unfamiliar woman exiting the café behind them.

"Oh, hi. I just saw her and wanted to say hello, that's all."

"I'm Emily, Amanda's friend." Emily stuck out her hand, which Snow shook.

"I'm Snow."

Emily's eyes widened. "Snow. I see." Emily looked her up and down.

Had Amanda been talking about her? It was clear that she'd said something. Emily was scrutinizing Snow carefully, as though trying to decide whether what she'd been told was true or not.

"Have you and Amanda been friends for long?"

"Ever since we were in college. She doesn't keep a lot of friends, but those of us who are in her circle are lucky to have her."

"What's she like?" Snow asked rather breathlessly. "To her old friends, I mean?"

Emily smiled. "Amanda is fiercely protective of those she loves. She never shies away from a fight, especially if it'll benefit her or something she cares for. It's one of the things that drew her and Nicole together—and also the very thing that ultimately drove them apart."

"Nicole?"

"Amanda's ex-wife. She left her around six months ago."

Snow felt a surge of sympathy for Amanda. Maybe that's why she had been so standoffish with Snow; she was hurting, still missing her ex-wife. Perhaps Snow had done something that reminded her of Nicole.

"I don't imagine she was very kind to you."

Snow looked up in surprise. "She said something?"

"Don't take it personally, Snow. Amanda is very competitive. She doesn't like anyone outshining her."

"The greeting cards," Snow realized. "She's angry with me because mine are doing so well?"

Emily nodded. "I'm sure she'll get over it eventually, but for now, know that you didn't see the best side of her. Amanda can be a real ass when she wants to be and I'm very sorry you got caught up in that. There are many more sides to Amanda."

Snow wished she could have seen some of those sides. She thought she might have caught a glimpse of one of them when she and Amanda had that intense moment together, as Snow was preparing her for a shot.

"I should get going. It was nice to meet you, Snow."

"You too, Emily. Thank you for helping me understand."

"I don't make a habit of talking about Amanda's private business, but you deserved an explanation for her shitty behaviour, not that it excuses it. But, I hope it helps."

"It does. Thank you again."

Snow waved as Emily got into her car. She realized that she was shivering; there was a biting wind coming up.

Snow supposed Amanda was heading home now. There was no point in staying here anymore. Still, it hadn't been a complete waste of time, coming here. She had learned a bit more about Amanda, and what Snow now knew only made her weird crush on Amanda stronger.

She went home and logged onto Facebook, navigating to Amanda's page. She saw that Amanda had already put up a number of the photos that Snow had taken.

Snow grinned and scrolled down, looking for her name.

It wasn't there.

She frowned and looked again. Nope, no photo credit. Had Amanda forgotten to credit her? Surely, that was the explanation. She wouldn't have left Snow's name off deliberately.

Snow fired off a quick email.

Hey, Amanda. I'm sure this is a mistake, but you've forgotten to credit me in the photos you posted. Snow.

There was no response. Snow refreshed the page, checking if Amanda had perhaps credited her and failed to respond to the email. Nope, nothing. Snow gritted her teeth. She had worked hard on those photos. They were her best work. She deserved to be credited for them.

It was one of the reasons why she worked with the agency—part of their agreement with clients was that the photographer would always be credited.

Snow could see Amanda responding to posts on her Facebook page. She was clearly online. She must have read Snow's email by now, but she was ignoring it.

It was so unfair. Snow wasn't easily given to anger, but now, she was furious. She wasn't going to put up with this. Just because Amanda had some irrational jealousy of Snow's success didn't mean she got to treat Snow like this.

Before she was fully aware of making the decision, Snow found herself in the car. She drove straight to Amanda's house, rehearsing arguments in her head. She was going to be calm and rational about this. She would remind Amanda of the agreement she had signed with the agency. She had to credit Snow; that's all there was to it.

Amanda took almost a minute to open the door and when she did, she stared blankly at Snow. "What are you doing here?"

"What am I doing here?" Snow tried to keep her anger in check, but it bubbled up through all of her defenses. "You know exactly what I'm doing here! Don't pretend you didn't get my email!"

It quickly became apparent that shouting was not the right approach with Amanda. "Don't you talk to me in that tone, girl! I gave you a job and you were well paid for it."

Snow tried to temper her tone, and failed. "You're supposed to credit me! That's part of the agreement with the agency."

"There are no legal documents saying that. The photos are my property now. Go cry to the agency if you want, they're not going to force the issue, not if they want to keep my business."

Snow's instinct was to retreat, to back down, but she fought it. Her anger helped. Amanda had no right to treat her this way.

"You signed an agreement, Amanda. It might not be a legal document but it is still an agreement. If you don't uphold your end, then the next person you hear from will be my lawyer. God, it's no wonder your wife left you!"

With that, Snow turned and stormed off into the field of trees.

No need to tell Amanda that she couldn't afford a lawyer. She was so mad that she didn't even feel bad about lying.

Snow walked quickly through the lines of fir trees. As the beauty of nature surrounded her, her anger faded.

It had probably been a mistake, coming here. Amanda was sure to complain about her to the agency, and how in the world was Snow going to explain herself? She had shown up at a client's house, shouted at her and stormed off in a huff. That wasn't going to go down well with her boss.

She deserved to be credited, but she should have approached it in a calmer manner. She should have contacted the agency about the problem rather than come to Amanda's house.

If she was being honest with herself, the credit issue wasn't the only reason Snow had come here. She had wanted to see Amanda again.

Clearly her heart was a fool. Why would she have a crush on someone so inconsiderate? She did, though. Amanda was so sexy when she was angry. Snow played back the expression on her face during the argument. Yes, definitely sexy.

Snow sighed and sat down on the ground, her back leaning against one of the trees. She'd stormed off in the wrong direction, of course. She'd have to pass the house to get back out of the Christmas tree field, unless she wanted to climb over the fence, which she definitely didn't want to do.

Maybe she could sneak past Amanda and avoid another confrontation. She needed to get out ahead of this. She'd call the agency and confess what had happened. They would ensure that Amanda gave her the credit she deserved for the photos.

Snow had been with the agency for years and knew that they looked out for the people who worked for them.

They wouldn't just let this slide. Snow would get her credit for the photos.

The thought of the photos had anger flaring up inside Snow once more. She didn't know if she was calm enough yet to walk past Amanda's house without going in to shout at her some more. Best to stay here for now, at least until she had cooled down a bit more. Then, she would go home and try to put this whole mess behind her.

Snow forced herself to look at her surroundings. The Christmas tree farm really was beautiful. Being outside in nature had always been a balm to her, but right now, she was still smoldering with resentment over the photos to enjoy it much.

She couldn't believe Amanda. Who would be that self-centered?

Who else could be so sexy while being utterly infuriating at the same time?

Snow felt like an idiot for having the stupid crush that she did. Trust her to fall for a woman who didn't respect her. Snow had never had good luck with relationships.

Such anger wasn't like Snow, and she didn't enjoy the feeling. She supposed that she felt betrayed by Amanda, given that Snow really liked her and Amanda had still gone behind her back, making it look as though she herself had taken the photos.

She had said some horrible things to Amanda, but she was too angry just now to regret them. She would probably feel bad when she went home later, but for now, Snow fumed quietly among the fir trees.

7

Amanda stared off after Snow, her mouth gaping open.

When was the last time someone had shouted at her like that?

When was the last time someone had stood up to her like that?

Amanda honestly couldn't remember. It was probably sometime during the end of her relationship with Nicole.

Though, by all rights, Amanda shouldn't have enjoyed what had happened, the argument had excited her, both mentally and physically.

When she'd first met Snow, she had thought her to be one of those people who just lets everyone walk all over them because they don't like confrontation. She had thought it would be easy to get one over on Snow.

She still suspected that Snow didn't like confrontation, but clearly, she could be pushed into it.

As much as she wanted to hate her, Amanda couldn't help but feel a grudging respect for Snow. She knew that she wasn't an easy person to stand up to, and yet Snow had done it in a most spectacular fashion.

Amanda wanted to fix this. She truly hadn't been fair to Snow and owed her an apology. She put on a jacket and closed the door behind her as she went out among the fir trees. She had seen Snow disappearing somewhere off this way.

It was interesting that Snow hadn't left the property, as she easily could have. Of course, it could just be a coincidence. Snow was angry and might well have stormed off in no particular direction, landing up among the Christmas trees by chance.

Still, Amanda couldn't help but wonder if Snow hadn't left for a reason. Maybe the argument had excited her as much as it had Amanda. Perhaps she was hoping it would continue.

Amanda had no intention of arguing further, however arousing the idea may be. She was going to apologize and promise to credit Snow in the photos. She knew she was in the wrong and it was time to stop being an ass about it.

Snow wasn't hard to find. She hadn't wandered far and was sitting with her back to one of the trees near the house. When Amanda approached, she leapt to her feet, glaring.

Amanda held her hands up in surrender. "I'm not here to fight. I just want to talk."

"There's nothing left to talk about," Snow spat.

"Yes, there is. I owe you an apology."

That brought Snow up short. "Yes, you do," she said stiffly.

"I'm sorry, Snow. I should never have posted those photos without crediting you. I own them, according to the agreement I signed, but according to the same agreement, I should have listed you as the photographer."

"And why didn't you? It's not my fault that my cards are getting more attention than yours, you know."

Snow looked so beautiful when she was angry. Her blonde hair was wild and messy and her blue eyes flashed dangerously. Amanda was already throbbing with desire and being with Snow was making that situation worse by the moment. She hadn't been this attracted to anyone since she first met Nicole.

Amanda's body reacted before her mind gave permission. She stepped forward and captured Snow's lips in a passionate kiss. Snow made a small squeak of surprise but didn't pull away. She hesitated for only a moment before she was kissing Amanda back.

Amanda ran her tongue over the seam of Snow's lips and Snow opened for her. Their tongues danced together, sending sparks of desire throughout Amanda's body.

She finally pulled away for air, panting. Snow's cheeks were flushed and her pupils dilated.

Amanda wanted to kiss her again, but before she could, Snow stumbled back. "I—I should go."

"I'll credit you!" Amanda promised to Snow's retreating back. "And whatever else you want. I can even cut you in on the profits."

Snow didn't turn or acknowledge Amanda's offer. Amanda stared after her, wondering what in the world had come over her.

Snow was far from her usual type. Amanda usually went for women closer to her own age. She preferred glamourous, femme women. Smart professional women were Amanda's type... weren't they?

Snow's simple style was far from glamorous, and

Amanda wouldn't say she was overtly femme, either. Snow was naturally beautiful, yet in every way, she was unpolished and it suited her.

Amanda had been so attracted to Snow that she hadn't been able to control herself. And Amanda usually prided herself on her self control.

After a few minutes, she pulled herself together enough to go back into the house. She immediately sat down at her computer and went to her Facebook page. She typed comments in every single photo, crediting Snow and commenting on what an amazing job she had done. Once she was finished with Facebook, Amanda did the same thing on her website.

Satisfied that she had finally done right by Snow, Amanda let her hand fall off the mouse as she lapsed into thought.

She was attracted to Snow; she had known that from the first moment Snow walked in here. Before today, she had had no emotions toward Snow except anger and resentment.

Now, things were different. Anger had been replaced with grudging respect, and Amanda wondered if there might be something more for her and Snow in the future.

Of course, Snow probably hated her now, and with good reason. Amanda wondered if Snow might take her up on her idea to share some of the profits. Amanda didn't need the money, and it would be a good excuse to spend more time with Snow, to explore what might be between them.

It would probably be awkward at first, what with how Amanda had kissed Snow out of nowhere, but after Nicole, she was no stranger to awkward situations.

Amanda found herself dialing Emily's number. Emily answered on the sixth ring. "Hey, Amanda."

"Hey, Ems. Do you have time to talk?"

"Of course. What's up?"

"It's Snow."

Emily sighed. "What did you do now?"

"Nothing! Well, not nothing, but nothing bad."

"Then why are you calling me in the middle of your workday?"

"Okay, so it might have been bad," Amanda admitted. The more she thought about it, the more she realized that it had, in fact, been a poor decision on her part.

She had kissed Snow so quickly that Snow hadn't had a chance to see what she was about to do and give her consent. No consent constituted sexual assault. Amanda felt sick. Had she just assaulted Snow?

Snow had seemed to enjoy the kiss, judging by how she had kissed her back, but perhaps Amanda had misread that. Maybe Snow was just trying to get away from her and Amanda had misinterpreted that as desire. She didn't even know if Snow was gay.

The statistics were sadly against her. There were far more straight women than gay or bi women in the world.

"Amanda? Hello, can you hear me?"

"What?"

"Can you still hear me?"

"I—yes, sorry. I just zoned out for a minute."

"Well? Are you going to tell me what happened?"

"Snow came to the house. She was angry about me not crediting her in the photos. We argued..."

Emily sighed. "You should have seen that one coming."

"You didn't meet her. She came across as so passive, I

never thought she had this kind of reaction in her."

"So you're complaining because she stood up for herself."

"No, I'm not complaining. I liked it. A bit too much, in fact."

"What do you mean?"

"I... I might have kissed her."

Emily burst out laughing.

"This isn't funny, Ems! This is serious. She could be filing charges against me as we speak."

Emily's laughter cut off very suddenly. "You mean she wasn't willing?"

"I don't know! The whole thing happened so fast. She kissed me back, that much I'm fairly certain of, but what if she was just doing it to get the kiss over and done with as fast as possible? What if she was afraid of me and wanted to kiss me back just so that I'd let her go? She's so much younger than me, I just worry I've crossed some kind of line."

"Well, from what you've told me, it doesn't sound like she was afraid. If she was willing to come to you and start a fight, she's probably not so scared of you that she would suffer a kiss she didn't want. I bet she would have slapped you if she hadn't wanted it. I did actually meet her, you know."

"You did?"

"Yeah, just after you left from our lunch date. I'm not sure what she was doing in the area, but we bumped into each other. I told her a little about you."

"Why would you do that?"

"I felt like she deserved an explanation. You haven't exactly been fair to her."

"I know. So, that's how she knew about Nicole?"

"She said something?"

"She said, 'It's no wonder your wife left you.'"

Emily whistled softly. "It sounds like she was really mad."

"And she has a right to be. I've credited her in the photos now. I even offered to share some of the profits with her."

"Then it sounds like you've done all you can."

"I don't know... Should I apologize to her about the kiss?"

"No, I don't think that's necessary. It sounded like she wanted it, from what you've described. You've already apologized for everything you need to apologize for."

Amanda nodded slowly. That was good to hear. "Thanks, Emily. I really needed to get out of my head for a minute."

"No problem. So, what are you going to do about Snow?"

"What can I do? She clearly hates me now, and for good reason."

"I wouldn't be so sure. You don't kiss someone back unless there's at least some small part of you that doesn't hate them."

Amanda wasn't so sure about that. "I don't suppose there's anything more I can do, regardless. Unless Snow decides to take me up on my offer to share the profits, in which case we'll be working together some more."

Amanda found that she liked that idea, but it probably wasn't an idea that would ever come to pass. Snow didn't strike Amanda as the kind of person to say yes to such an offer.

She could only hope that in the future, her and Snow's paths would cross again.

8

S now was in shock. She drove on autopilot, heading home without really thinking about it. Her mind was full of Amanda's kiss.

Why had Amanda kissed her? Had she recognized Snow's pitiful crush and decided to play with her?

No, Snow didn't believe that of her. Yes, Amanda had failed to credit her in the photos, which was wrong, but it was a far cry from playing with a person's heart in that manner.

Perhaps Amanda had kissed Snow to try to make up for her behavior? It would be a strange thing to do, but Snow had seen plenty of strange things in her life.

No, she didn't think that had been it, either. The kiss had been too passionate for that.

That left only one option: Amanda was as attracted to Snow as Snow was to her. It was an intoxicating thought.

She was so distracted with thoughts of Amanda that she almost missed Bluebell's bus. Snow practically ran to the bus stop to be there when Bluebell got off.

"Are you okay, Mom? You look funny."

Snow chuckled. "I'm fine, sweetheart. I was just a bit late, so I had to hurry to get here."

"I can walk home by myself," Bluebell pouted. "I'm a big girl."

"That you are, but I want to spend time with you. I'll always want to spend time with you, no matter how big you are."

Bluebell seemed to find this answer satisfactory. She started chattering away about her day at school. All thoughts of Amanda left Snow's mind as she enjoyed spending time with her daughter. They were doing a new science section—this one with magnets and iron shavings.

Snow had never really liked science in school, but Bluebell loved it. She was so smart; Snow was sure that she could be a bigshot scientist one day if she wanted to. She had a small college fund for Bluebell that should be enough to get her somewhere decent as long as she earned a scholarship to pay for part of the fees.

"How about we stop by the store on the way home? I can buy us ingredients to make cupcakes."

"Ooh, can we make planet cupcakes?"

Snow chuckled. "Sure. We'll have to see what the store has in terms of decorations, but we can sort something out. You'll need to tell me what each planet looks like."

Snow knew what the different planets in the solar system looked like, but she loved listening to Bluebell describe them anyway. There was such enthusiasm in her voice that Snow couldn't help getting enthusiastic too.

They spent about half an hour at the store, selecting different toppings that could be made to look like the different planets. It was more money than Snow usually spent on baking, but she couldn't say no to Bluebell's planet idea, not when she was clearly so excited about it.

When they got home, Bluebell went dashing through the house and dragged Daisy through to the kitchen by her hand. Daisy sighed good-naturedly and helped Bluebell get out all the bowls and measuring cups.

"What brought this on?" Daisy gestured to the baking ingredients.

Snow shrugged. "I just thought it would be nice to make cupcakes together."

"Good call. I haven't seen Bluebell this excited since that volcano in science."

Snow could tell that her mother didn't quite believe her. Daisy always knew when something was on Snow's mind, but Snow didn't want to discuss it in front of Bluebell. In fact, she wasn't sure if she wanted to discuss it at all.

She still hadn't quite gotten her head around it. Did Amanda's kiss mean that Amanda liked her too, or had it simply been meant to shut her up? After all, it *had* done that. Snow had been effectively silenced by shock and had left before that shock had time to wear off.

Snow shook her head slightly, trying to focus on the task at hand. She was making cupcakes with Bluebell. She wanted to enjoy this time with her mother and daughter. She would think more about Amanda later.

The cupcakes were mostly a success. Jupiter ended up a bit of a mess, but Bluebell was happy, at least. Snow took several photos of the cupcakes, and then some of Bluebell posing with them. Bluebell also insisted on a family shot of the three of them, all holding cupcakes.

Snow made Bluebell help clean up the kitchen before

they all sat down together and had the cupcakes with a cup of tea.

Bluebell told Snow and Daisy some more about school and barely complained at all when Snow told her it was time to do her homework. Snow helped here and there, but for the most part, Bluebell knew what she was doing. Snow just had to check off in her homework diary that Bluebell had done everything.

Bluebell got out her new doll, the one Snow had bought her recently, and started playing with it. Snow kept an eye on her from the other room, but Bluebell didn't seem to require or desire her presence for now. She was off in her own world, narrating some game in her head as she moved the doll around.

"What's bothering you, Snow?"

Of course, Daisy could tell it was something. Snow glanced once more at Bluebell, who didn't appear to be listening to the conversation.

"It's Amanda."

"That rude woman you did the shoot for the other day?"

"Yes, that's her. She didn't credit me for the photos when she was supposed to. I got mad and went over to her house."

"You got mad?"

"Those were the best photos I've ever taken. I was just so inspired by her and how beautiful she is... anyway, we had a fight. Afterward, she came to apologize, but I was still angry and she kissed me."

Daisy raised an eyebrow. "Well, that's not what I was expecting."

"Me neither. I don't know how to feel about it."

"What do you mean? I thought you said she was really

rude to you? You were having a fight. You clearly didn't want a kiss. She had no right to kiss you. You should be furious. You could even press charges, if you want to."

"The thing is… I kind of did want her to," Snow admitted.

Daisy's eyebrow traveled further toward her hairline.

"I know she's a bit of an ass, but I think I've developed a crush on her. No, I know I have. I'm not sure why. She's just so sexy and confident, and I'm drawn to her like a moth to a candle."

"An apt description."

"You think this is a bad idea."

"What is *this*, exactly?"

"I don't know. Up until today, I thought my crush was going nowhere, but now I'm not sure. If she feels the same, do I pursue something with her?"

"From what you've told me, it doesn't sound like a good idea. It sounds like you will get burnt."

"I know, I know. She hasn't made the best first impression. But I believe that under all that, she's a good person."

"What makes you think that?"

"Just a feeling I have. You know I'm usually good at judging character."

"You are," Daisy conceded. "Look, if you like her, and you think you have a chance at a good future with her, then you should pursue that. Follow your heart, Snow. If your heart leads you to Amanda, then that's where you should go."

Snow bit her lip, thinking. "I'm not even sure how I'd go about it. What if the kiss was just a one-time thing? What if she didn't like it and doesn't want a repeat experience? She may not want to see me again."

"Well, that's the risk you take. You have her number,

don't you? You can give her a call, if you'd like. Or, you could wait and see if she contacts you. She may be having much the same thoughts as you are."

Snow hadn't thought of that, but Daisy was right. Perhaps waiting would be the smarter move. Amanda seemed like a woman who went for what she wanted. If she wanted to see Snow again, she would make sure Snow knew it.

"Thanks, Mom. It helps to talk things out."

"I know, honey. Why don't you take some time to think? I can watch Bluebell for a bit."

"Thanks. I think I will."

Snow took a long walk, which did wonders for her spinning mind. She decided that she would wait and see what happened with Amanda. If it was meant to be, then it would be.

That night, Snow lay in bed after her mom and Bluebell were asleep, thinking back to the kiss. She had been with women before, but none of her relationships had ever seemed to work out. She had kissed and been kissed, but none of it had ever been as hot as that steamy kiss Amanda had given her.

Snow remembered the feeling of Amanda's tongue in her mouth. It had felt so divine and yet not enough. She needed more, but she had fled before she got to find out if Amanda had more in mind.

In her imagination, Snow didn't flee the confrontation. She stayed and let Amanda kiss her. Snow's lips parted as she imagined Amanda deepening the kiss, maybe pulling Snow close so that their bodies were pressed up against each other.

Snow checked that the door was closed before she wet her fingers with spit and snuck a hand between her legs. It had been too long since she had done this. Between her work and raising Bluebell, even with her mom's help, she had little time for self-pleasure.

She should probably be going to sleep, but Snow was too turned on by the thought of Amanda doing filthy things to her to be tired right now. She ran a finger lightly over her clit, biting back a soft moan.

Snow spread her legs and started slipping her wet fingers over her clitoris. She rubbed lightly at first, up and down, then harder in circles just over the hood. Snow dipped a further downward, scooping up some wetness from her pussy and using it to smooth the path of her fingers over her clit.

She imagined Amanda's hand here instead. What would it feel like? Would Amanda be rough or gentle? Would she go fast or take her time?

Snow remembered the feeling of Amanda's tongue in her mouth and moved her hand faster over her clit. She was close to release now, her thoughts filled with Amanda, Amanda's tongue, Amanda's hands, Amanda's breath on her cheek.

Snow bit her lip as she came, stifling her cry. She shuddered through the orgasm, gasping for breath.

Snow's eyes fluttered closed as the final aftershocks faded.

She couldn't believe she had just gotten off to the thought of Amanda. What would Amanda say if she knew? Snow wondered if Amanda might get herself off to thoughts of the kiss, the same as she had. Amanda had certainly seemed to enjoy it.

She forcibly shut down those thoughts, not because they weren't blindingly pleasant, but because if she kept this up, she'd need another round before she could sleep.

She wiped her hand on the sheet, making a mental note to change it tomorrow morning. For now, she needed to rest.

Snow finally drifted off, sleepy and sated after the best orgasm she'd had in a while. When she dreamed, her dreams were of Amanda.

9

Amanda woke with a gasp. She felt between her legs and realized she was wet. Of course she was. Her dream about Snow had been so hot that it followed her into her waking life.

She slipped a hand between her legs. She was barely awake, but she was awake enough to feel desire. Amanda touched herself to the thought of Snow. Snow's lips had felt so good against hers; so right. Their kiss had been too short. She wished that Snow would have stayed longer, but Amanda couldn't blame her for leaving.

The way she had approached the kiss was all wrong. She should have taken Snow on a proper date and kissed her goodnight at the door.

Somehow, she couldn't bring herself to regret it, no matter how logical it would be. It was the best kiss she'd ever had—and Nicole was an excellent kisser. There was just something so sweet and innocent about Snow that added a level of wonder to the kiss that Amanda hadn't felt in a long time.

Amanda replaced her right hand with her wand

vibrator from her bedside drawer and held it against her clit as she filled her mind with images of Snow, remembering the wonderful feeling of Snow's slick tongue dancing with hers.

Amanda moaned loudly as she came, squirting all over her bedding.

Oh well. The sheets had needed to be changed anyway.

She dearly wished that she could go back to sleep, but she was awake now, and the bed wasn't nearly as comfortable as it had been a few minutes ago, given that the portion in the middle was now wet.

Amanda rolled out of bed and changed the sheets, yawning. She made herself a breakfast of bacon and eggs. Amanda looked around the empty kitchen as she ate. How she wished there was someone here to enjoy breakfast with her. She was lonely, but she didn't feel like going on Tinder right now. She was beginning to think that the app was more trouble than it was worth.

Amanda wondered how Snow would look in her kitchen. Beautiful, no doubt. Did Snow like bacon and eggs? Could they share this breakfast together?

Amanda snorted. Yeah, she was lonely, alright. She barely knew Snow. It was one thing having lusty thoughts about her but quite another having tender, domestic thoughts.

She supposed that it was to be expected. It had been six months since Nicole left, after all. Of course her brain was latching on to anyone who had a chance of making her feel less alone.

Amanda forced her mind away from Snow as she finished breakfast and sat down at her computer. She scrolled through some of the comments, grinning. The photos Snow had taken were going down even better than she had imagined.

Amanda replied to several questions and printed out about fifteen copies of photos on her high-quality printer, straight onto stiff card so that she could just cut them out and fold them before sending them off.

Amanda spent the next hour or so lining up cards in the guillotine, making sure that she cut them exactly straight. Once she was happy with the cards, she put them in envelopes and addressed them. She would have to make a stop at the post office to send these later today.

Amanda found herself staring once more at the beautiful pictures Snow had taken. She couldn't help but wonder what a photo of the two of them kissing in front of the Christmas trees would have looked like. She bet it would be all kinds of hot.

It took a bit of searching, but Amanda was able to track down Snow's personal Facebook page. Amanda felt her eyes widen in surprise as she found pictures of Snow and her daughter—Bluebell, the captions named her. Of course Snow would have a daughter called Bluebell. It looked like her mother was named Daisy. Someone needed to teach this family about proper naming conventions.

She didn't see anyone who might be Bluebell's father in any of the photos. Maybe he was out of the picture? Amanda certainly hoped that Snow wasn't with anyone at the moment. Is Snow bisexual? Is she gay? Is she straight? Facebook wasn't making it clear.

Snow wouldn't have kissed Amanda back if she was already in a relationship, though. She wasn't the type to cheat. Amanda didn't know her very well yet, but she was sure that Snow would be faithful to whoever she chose.

Bluebell was adorable. She had the same blonde hair and blue eyes as Snow, she looked exactly like her mom. Amanda wondered what it might be like to have some family photos as part of her Christmas card line. They were doing so well and she felt so inspired by the photos that Snow had taken.

Yes, a few family shots would be amazing. It would add a homey feel to the cards and open up the target market to larger families.

Of course, there was only one person who she wanted to take the photos. Snow's previous work had been so amazing, Amanda would be crazy not to use her.

A small part of her wondered how much of her idea was purely to capitalize on the Christmas market and how much came from wanting to see Snow again.

Amanda told herself that seeing Snow again was just a fortunate side effect of what was a very good, business-oriented decision. If she told herself that enough times, she might start actually believing it.

She considered contacting the agency again, but decided to go straight to Snow. It felt less impersonal, calling her directly rather than through a middleman.

Amanda scrolled through her emails until she found Snow's number, which the agency had provided the first time they sent Snow.

She hesitated, her finger over the dial button.

This was ridiculous. There was no reason for her to be nervous phoning Snow. She was proposing a business transaction, nothing more. Snow would take the photos, and Amanda would pay her. Simple.

Before they went ahead, though, she wanted to get Snow's ideas. As much as she didn't like to admit it, Snow had amazing ideas and an eye for things, much more than

Amanda did. She prided herself on her business acumen and was relatively confident in her ability to take a good photo, but she was nowhere near Snow's level at seeing the beauty in things.

She didn't understand how Snow wasn't better known, given the quality of her work. Amanda supposed that much of it depended on luck. She certainly wouldn't be as successful as she was without a healthy dose of luck in her early days of running a business, when she was struggling to put herself on the map.

Amanda pressed dial. The phone rang eight times before Snow answered. "Hello?"

"Hello, Snow. This is Amanda Asher."

There was silence on the other end of the line.

Amanda pressed onward. "I was hoping I could hire you for a consultation. I would like to discuss an idea I have for some photographs that I want taken for my Christmas cards."

"I—yes. Of course! I'd love to do a consultation for you." Snow sounded flustered, but not unenthusiastic. "How does tomorrow morning sound? I could come over at nine."

"Tomorrow morning at nine is perfect. Thank you, Snow. I will see you then."

"See you then, Amanda."

Snow hung up, leaving Amanda with a silly smile on her face. She genuinely wanted Snow's advice on her idea, but she also wanted to see Snow. This was the perfect excuse. She could gauge whether Snow was interested in doing something more than kissing her, or if she thought the whole thing had been a mistake and wanted nothing more than a professional relationship.

Amanda spent the rest of the day wondering how she

was going to approach her meeting with Snow. Would she mention the kiss? No, it was probably best to take her cues from Snow. If Snow wanted to talk about it, they would, but Amanda didn't want to drag the subject up if Snow would prefer to forget about it.

She went online and stated searching Christmas cards with family photos on them. Amanda had to admit, they looked amazing. She thought that she could create some great family shots among her Christmas trees with her fake snow machine.

She went to bed that night with her mind buzzing with ideas. Amanda couldn't wait to discuss them with Snow the next day.

As to what the next day would bring for their relationship, Amanda could do nothing but wait and see.

S now dressed carefully the next morning. She knew that it was probably stupid, but she wanted to look good when she saw Amanda. She even considered makeup, but in the end decided that it would be overkill. She knew that women like Amanda wore makeup every day, but that just wasn't Snow's style.

She ended up in a long-sleeved blue dress with little white snowflakes around the sleeves and bottom hem. It would match perfectly with Amanda's snow machine. Not that Snow was going to be in the photos, but she hoped that Amanda would find her pretty.

"Snow, I've got to go. A client has just called. They're interested in buying ten of my paintings!"

Daisy's eyes were shining with enthusiasm, and Snow was happy for her, she truly was, but she still had to bite back a groan. "I've got my meeting with Amanda. Who's going to watch Bluebell?"

Daisy bit her lip. "We could take her over to Mrs. Johnson?"

"I'm not leaving her with Mrs. Johnson. She smokes all the time, and that isn't good for Bluebell's lungs."

"I could stay," Daisy said slowly. "Maybe the client would be willing to reschedule the meeting."

Snow knew that ten paintings was a huge sale that would make a big difference for their family. "No, you don't want to jeopardize your sale. You go ahead. I'll make a plan."

"Are you sure?"

"I am. Good luck."

"Thanks, Snow. I'll see you later."

Snow gave brief thought to postponing her meeting with Amanda, but was too eager to see her again to consider that for long.

"Bluebell, get dressed. We're going out."

Bluebell was soon dressed in a bright red coat and purple pants, with a purple knitted hat on her head. "Where are we going, Mom?"

"I'm taking you to work with me. We're going to see a nice woman called Amanda who has a Christmas Tree farm."

At least, Snow hoped Amanda was nice. She hadn't been very nice so far, but Snow liked to think that things would be different after the kiss. She had checked, and Amanda had indeed credited her for her work. Snow hoped that the problems Amanda had had with her in the beginning were no longer an issue for Amanda.

She certainly didn't want Amanda upsetting Bluebell. If she did, Snow would be out of there in an instant and she wouldn't be returning. No one hurt her daughter. No one.

She was nervous as she knocked on Amanda's door.

It opened almost immediately.

Amanda looked spectacular in a long pale blue dress with a puffy dark blue jacket over it. Her makeup was done impeccably and her lovely chocolate brown hair was styled to look like it was caught in the middle of a gust of wind.

"Well, hello, there." Amanda's eyes were drawn to Bluebell. "What's your name?"

"Bluebell." Bluebell's eyes remained shyly on the ground.

"That's a wonderful name," Amanda said warmly. "Why don't you come inside, Bluebell." She held out a hand, which Bluebell took eagerly. Amanda smiled at Snow as she led Bluebell into the house.

"I didn't know you were bringing company." She didn't sound unhappy, just curious.

"My mom had to go out and there was no one to watch Bluebell. I hope it's okay that I brought her."

"Of course. I love children. It'll be my pleasure to host Bluebell for our meeting. Why don't we go through to the lounge?"

Snow beamed as Amanda took Bluebell to one of the couches and gave her a doll to play with.

"It's one of my props for my Christmas photos," Amanda explained. "I want to do some with Christmas trees surrounded by presents, some of which have been opened."

"That sounds great! Is that the idea you wanted to discuss?"

"No, I actually wanted to discuss branching out a little. What do you think of cards with family photos on them?"

Snow thought about this for a moment. "I think that could work really well. Christmas is a family time, after all, and it'll give your cards a homier feel. We'll need to set up the lighting carefully—make it nice and cozy."

"Great! I was thinking we could do them outside, but if you want cozier lightning, we could bring one of the trees into the lounge and pose there."

"That'll be perfect. Do you have a family to model for you yet?"

"Not yet. I hadn't thought that far in advance. I just wanted to discuss it with you first to see what you thought."

Snow glowed internally to hear how Amanda valued her opinion. This Amanda was certainly different to the angry, difficult woman Snow had met the first time.

"Well, we can take some test shots in the meantime, just to show you a concept idea while you're looking for a family to model for you. I've got a distance shutter for the camera. You and I can pose with Bluebell as a test family."

"Oh, I don't know... maybe it'll be better to wait until I have a family I've paid to model."

"We don't mind at all, do we, Bluebell? You want to be in some photos, honey?"

Bluebell leaped up from her chair. "Yes, please!" She struck a pose, just as Snow had taught her.

"You have a young model in the making," Amanda said seriously, her eyes twinkling as she watched Bluebell. Snow blushed and smiled. There was no quicker way to her heart than through her daughter.

"Come on, I'll help you get one of the Christmas trees in here. Bluebell, you just wait here for a few minutes. We'll be ready to take the photos soon."

Amanda and Snow managed to get one of the smaller Christmas trees into the lounge with a bare minimum of mess. Snow brushed some pine needles off her dress and was grateful that it hadn't been anything worse.

Snow set up her camera and held the distance shutter hidden in the back of her hand. "Okay, Bluebell, come and stand between us. Yes, just like that. Amanda, can I put my arm around you?"

"Of course."

Amanda stood slightly closer, and Snow hesitantly snaked an arm around her waist. Amanda did the same thing with her. It felt surprisingly intimate to be standing together like this, with Bluebell innocently between them.

Snow smiled into the camera and took a few shots.

"Alright, let's get us sitting around the Christmas tree. Bluebell, if you could sit there. Here, take this present and put it on your lap. Amanda, sit like this. I'm going to lean against you, okay?"

"Okay." Amanda sounded slightly breathless, but she wrapped her arms around Snow as Snow leaned her back against Amanda's chest. She felt Amanda's breasts pressing against her back.

Snow gazed at Bluebell, letting all the love for her daughter show on her face. She then turned to Amanda, staring into her forest green eyes and taking a few photos like that.

"How about we do a few outside?" Amanda suggested. "The lighting won't be as cozy, but it'll look so beautiful with the snow falling around us."

"Great idea! Those last photos in the snow did look incredible."

Amanda leaned down to speak to Bluebell on her level. "Are you warm enough to go outside, sweety? Do you want another jacket?"

Bluebell shook her head. "No, thank you."

"At least take this scarf. It'll look lovely on you."

Amanda took a small cashmere scarf from where it was hanging over the back of a couch. It did look wonderful on Bluebell, the blue matching her eyes perfectly. Bluebell stroked the scarf reverently. "It's so soft. I've never felt anything this soft before."

Amanda beamed at her. "You can keep it. It looks better on you than on me anyway."

"Amanda, you don't have to…"

"I know I don't have to, but I want to. Consider it my Christmas gift to Bluebell."

Bluebell squealed in delight and threw her arms around Amanda. "Thank you, Amanda! It's the best Christmas gift ever. I'll take such good care of it."

"I'm sure you will, honey. Now come on, bundle up. Let's get those outside photos done." Amanda exchanged a warm smile with Snow before leading the way out onto the Christmas tree farm.

Amanda turned on the snow machine while Snow and Bluebell got settled in front of one of the more impressive Christmas trees. Amanda sat down on the ground with them, letting Snow rest her head against Amanda's shoulder while Bluebell played in the snow.

They did a few shots like that before Snow brought up her next idea. "There's one more thing…"

"What is it?"

"You don't have to do this if you don't feel comfortable, but I think it would make for a great shot."

"Out with it, Snow. Your ideas are pure genius. If you think it'll make a good shot, then we're doing it."

"We should pose for a kiss. It doesn't have to be a real kiss. We'll just need to have our lips touching for the camera."

Amanda looked taken aback for only a moment. "That would make a good photo," she agreed. There was a faint hint of red to her cheeks, but no other outward sigh of discomfort.

"We don't have to do it..."

"No, I want to. Should we have Bluebell in that shot?"

"I think so. Is it okay if she opens some of those prop presents you have?"

"Of course. The boxes are empty, but I can always rewrap them afterward."

"Bluebell, honey, won't you go inside and grab some of those boxes."

Bluebell, who seemed to think this was all great fun, got up and dashed inside.

Snow carefully arranged herself and Amanda so that they would be in the perfect position for the camera. When Bluebell returned with the boxes, Snow directed her to sit at her and Amanda's feet and start opening them slowly.

Snow leaned very close to Amanda. "When I give the word, press your lips to mine. Smile and close your eyes."

"I'm ready," Amanda breathed.

"Now." Snow's voice was every bit as breathy as Amanda's.

Their lips touched. Snow almost forgot to press the distance shutter for the camera, but fortunately she remembered at the last moment. She snapped a few more shots, which maybe weren't strictly necessary, just to prolong the feeling of Amanda's lips on hers.

She regretfully pulled back. Amanda's eyes fluttered open, and they were starting at each other, both lost for words. Even though they hadn't kissed properly, it felt more intimate than the kiss they had shared the other day. Less hot, but more intimate.

"I think we're done."

Snow didn't think she was imagining the disappointment mirrored on Amanda's face. She felt the same, but she couldn't justify taking up any more of Amanda's day. This was a professional visit, after all. She needed to keep that in mind.

"Thank you, Snow."

"Tell me when you've found a family to model and I'll come and take the proper shots."

"I think you just have."

Snow glowed internally. She had just meant for these to be practice shots, but she loved that Amanda liked them so much she would use them on her Christmas cards.

"If you agree, that is. Are you happy for you and Bluebell to be on my Christmas cards?"

"What do you think, Bluebell? Do you want to be on a Christmas card?"

"Ooh, Mom, please, can I? That would be so cool!"

Snow grinned. "You heard her. Sign us up."

"Thank you, Snow. I'll make sure to credit you properly from the start this time."

"Thank you." Snow tried to think of a reason to stay for longer, but she was coming up blank. She'd taken all the shots she could think of for this particular project. "I should get going."

"I—do you want a cup of tea?"

Snow beamed. "I'd love one."

"I have hot chocolate, too, with marshmallows. Are you interested, Bluebell?"

"Yes, please! Can I, Mom?"

"One mug."

Bluebell squealed in excitement. "I can help you make it, Amanda. I know how to make my own hot chocolate now."

"I would certainly appreciate the help." Amanda held out a hand for Bluebell's and led her into the kitchen.

Snow could hear them chatting happily as they made the tea and hot chocolate. Bluebell told Amanda all about school and her friends. Amanda was attentive and seemed genuinely interested in what Bluebell had to say.

Snow had never guessed that Amanda might be so taken with Bluebell. This whole day had turned out so much better than she could have hoped, even in her most optimistic imaginings.

A few minutes later, Amanda returned with three mugs. She sat Bluebell down before handing her the mug of hot chocolate, adorned with mini marshmallows on top.

"Thanks, Amanda." Snow took a sip of her tea, which was delicious. It tasted faintly of something like cinnamon.

There were a few minutes of silence, but it didn't feel awkward. The three of them each sipped on their drinks, immersed in their own thoughts.

"How are your Christmas cards going, Snow? Are they still getting as much attention as they did at first?"

Amanda didn't sound resentful, merely curious.

"Yeah, they're really taking off. I've been running around getting stuff printed and posted. I've never gotten this many orders before."

"You deserve them. You're incredibly talented. It's a wonder that it's taken people this long to notice it."

Snow felt herself blushing again. The fact that a

successful businesswoman like Amanda thought she was extremely talented warmed her from the inside. It gave her hope for the future of her work. Maybe this big break was all she needed to start making the kinds of sales she hoped to make one day.

"I'm hoping to get my own printer soon. It'll be a good investment, I think."

"It certainly will be. I've gotten endless use out of my printer. Have you decided on a brand yet?"

They chatted for almost an hour. Amanda gave Snow some good advice on which printer brands to get, and Snow found out some more about Amanda's business history.

She certainly had a talent for business, judging by how well she seemed to be doing. Snow picked up several useful tips from her, and in turn gave Amanda advice on how to improve her photography skills.

Bluebell whined when they had to leave. "Just five more minutes..."

"I told Grandma that we'd join her for lunch. You wouldn't want to miss her macaroni cheese, now would you?"

Bluebell brightened. "Macaroni cheese is the best!"

"I know it is, honey." Snow turned to Amanda. "Thanks for this, Amanda. We—we could do it again sometime, if you'd like?"

"I'd love that. Can I Whatsapp you?"

"Absolutely."

Snow was grinning widely all the way home.

now sent Amanda the photos the next day. Amanda was practically vibrating with excitement as she opened them.

They were even more spectacular than she had imagined, and she had set her expectations pretty high.

She, Snow and Bluebell looked like such a happy little family. It made Amanda wonder if she and Nicole had been wrong not to have children. They had both been so focused on their business that they had judged they wouldn't have enough time to devote to a child.

Meeting Bluebell made Amanda wonder if she was too old to be a parent. She assumed she couldn't get pregnant anymore, but that didn't mean she couldn't adopt, or have someone act as surrogate for her.

She wouldn't want to do it alone, though. Amanda didn't want to give up her business, which meant she would need a partner to help in childcare. She could get a nanny, of course, but that was no replacement for the care of a parent.

No, perhaps it was too late for her.

Amanda couldn't wait to see Snow and Bluebell again.

Her thoughts drifted to Snow. She looked so beautiful in the photos. Amanda wished that she had kissed Snow again when she last saw her, but she hadn't wanted to do so in front of Bluebell.

Amanda scrolled through the photos again, trying to pick her favorite one. It was a difficult choice.

Of course, this opened up a whole new world of possibilities. These photos would appeal to an LGBT audience, which would be amazing. Amanda had never geared her stuff specifically toward that community before, but now that the opportunity arose, she found that she liked the idea a lot.

She wondered if she might need to take some more photos with Snow. Maybe if these greeting cards sold well, she could justify another shoot. Amanda remembered how intimate it had felt posing with Snow, and how much she had wanted to properly kiss her.

Though she'd seen her only a day ago, Amanda already wanted another excuse to see Snow.

She couldn't believe how much she liked Snow now, after hating her at first. Amanda felt ashamed of the way she had behaved toward Snow in the beginning, but judging by how things went yesterday, Snow didn't hold it against her. Nicole would have taken that sort of grudge to her grave, but Snow wasn't like that.

Amanda lost herself in her work, designing the perfect Christmas cards with the photos Snow had sent her. It wasn't difficult. The photos were so good that the cards practically made themselves.

Once she was done, Amanda stepped away from her computer to get some fresh air. She always found that coming back to check her work after a little walk helped her pick up tiny mistakes she may have missed.

Amanda strolled through the fir trees, humming under her breath. She wandered over to the tree where she had first kissed Snow. They had both been angry then, but the kiss had been so hot that it had overwhelmed Amanda's anger completely.

Amanda didn't dwell on the kiss for too long. If she did, she knew that she would have to get herself off again, and she had no intention of doing so outside among the trees.

She wondered what it would feel like to press Snow up against one of the trees and take her from behind.

No, Amanda. Work thoughts, not sexy thoughts.

Of course, going back to work didn't do much to dispel her sexy thoughts, given that the pictures she was working with were all of Snow looking so beautiful and kissable that Amanda could barely contain her fantasies.

With a sigh of surrender, she leaned back in her chair and reached a hand between her legs.

Amanda thought of Snow as she rubbed her clit. She didn't do anything to draw it out. She was meant to be working, after all.

The pressure built quickly, and Amanda cried out Snow's name as she came hard, squirting right through her pants and onto the chair beneath her.

Amanda felt herself blushing, even though there was no one here to see. She didn't always squirt when she came, but when she was thinking of Snow, she just couldn't seem to help herself.

It wasn't always the most convenient thing, always requiring some kind of clean up.

Amanda shuffled to the bathroom grabbing a new set

of pants and panties as she did so. She cleaned herself up and got changed before coming back to clean her chair and the floor around it. Not only had she squirted again, but she'd squirted *a lot*. Really, what had gotten into her recently?

Amanda knew the answer to that. Snow had gotten into her. Ha, she wished. Or more like she wished she'd gotten into Snow. Amanda imagined pressing her fingers into Snow's welcoming body and forcibly shoved the thought from her mind. One new pair of pants was plenty for one day.

Once she was sure that she was happy with her greeting cards, Amanda started posting them on her website. She made a new sub-page of her website for her special range of family Christmas cards. Amanda wondered about doing personalized Christmas cards for clients. She had the snow machine and her Christmas tree farm.

It was an extremely popular idea. People loved sending photocards to family and friends at the holidays. Amanda was surprised she didn't think of this earlier. She needed to discuss it with Snow. She would get Snow to take the photos, of course. It could be a good reason to see her.

Amanda wondered if Snow was thinking of her the same way Amanda was thinking of Snow. She hoped so. Snow had seemed to enjoy their tea together. Amanda wondered if she should ask Snow out on a date, but she didn't feel like she could do so yet without a proper excuse to see Snow.

She would have to think of something, because not seeing Snow again was not an option.

12

Snow was midway through helping Bluebell with her homework when her phone pinged. She didn't pay much attention to it until she saw the name on the screen. It was Amanda.

Hey, Snow. I was thinking, I would like to split the proceeds for the family photo Christmas cards with you.

Snow responded at once.

You don't need to do that. You already paid me for the photoshoot—very generously, I may add.

Amanda had paid almost double Snow's standard rate. Snow had thought it was a mistake, but when she had asked for Amanda's bank details to transfer back the extra, Amanda had told her that she had deliberately left a tip. It was a huge 'tip', but Snow wasn't complaining.

This, though, was too much.

I know, but these things are selling so well that it seems only fair that you get a portion of the income. After all, I may have had the idea, but without you and Bluebell, that idea never would have come to fruition.

That wasn't strictly true. Amanda could easily have

gotten another photographer, but Snow knew that the photos she had taken for Amanda were wonderful. Another photographer could have also taken beautiful images, but that didn't necessarily mean they would be as good as the shots Snow had managed to get.

I don't know... are you sure?

Absolutely. Use the money to buy Bluebell something nice for Christmas.

Snow grinned. She loved how fond Amanda seemed to be of Bluebell.

I will do that, then. Thank you, Amanda.

Snow hesitated. She wanted to see Amanda again, and this was the perfect opportunity. She wasn't usually this forward, but she really wanted to see Amanda again.

Would you like to meet up sometime? To celebrate the success of the cards?

Yeah, that would be great! Tomorrow?

Snow breathed a sigh of relief. So, she wasn't being too forward, then.

Tomorrow is perfect. Do you have a place in mind?

How about Tanner's, down the road from my house?

Tanner's was fancier than the kinds of places Snow usually went to, but she wasn't worried. She still had Amanda's large tip, and she would soon have half of the profits from the Christmas cards. She couldn't believe Amanda was being so kind and generous.

Amanda had made a horrible first impression, but her recent actions had more than made up for it. Snow was so glad that she knew her and got the chance to work for with her.

Tanner's is perfect. Shall we say at three?

Three is great. I'll see you then.

See you, Amanda.

Snow expected that to be the end of their exchange, but a moment later, her phone pinged again.

I keep thinking of you when I see the snow. You're more beautiful, though.

Snow found herself blushing and was glad that she was alone in the room. *I don't know about that. I fear I'm no match for that automated snow machine you have.*

I wouldn't mind comparing sometime... though to be fair, the snow machine isn't wearing clothes, so I'm not sure I would be able to make an accurate comparison.

Snow giggled.

Is that you way of trying to get me naked?

I confess nothing...

I wonder what kind of things you might confess, if I got you flustered enough?

That wouldn't be difficult.

That was news to Snow. Amanda always seemed so cool and collected, Snow never would have guessed that Amanda was just as affected by her presence as Snow was by hers.

They flirted back and forth for a bit through Whatsapp. Snow could barely believe this was happening. She never would have thought that someone like Amanda would be interested in her in this way, but Amanda was making it clear that she was.

The kiss hadn't just been about shutting Snow up, then. Amanda really liked her. The long chat they had had over tea after the photoshoot should have proven that, but Snow had still been uncertain. Now, she wasn't anymore.

She wondered if their upcoming celebration tomorrow counted as a date. She hoped so.

Snow dressed carefully the next day. She wasn't sure if

this was a date or not, but regardless, she wanted to look good for Amanda.

When she arrived at Tanner's, Amanda was looking stunning, as always, with her hair done up in an elegant knot on the top of her head, in a pair of tight red pants with a dark green top that matched her eyes. She looked very Christmasy and was the picture of pure sexiness.

Snow sat down opposite her, feeling slightly breathless. "Hi."

"Hi, Snow. How are you?"

"I'm good! I've had a lot of work to do recently, what with my cards and people who heard about the award wanting to hire me for photoshoots."

"I suppose I should be grateful that I wasn't put on a waiting list."

"I do have a waiting list," Snow admitted. "I know the boss, though. I managed to pull some strings with her."

Amanda chuckled. "Glad to hear I'm in good standing with her."

"You are. How about you? The cards with the photos we took seem to be selling spectacularly." Snow had received a transfer to her account already and was shocked by the amount—but pleased nonetheless.

"Yes, they've been doing wonderfully! Your ideas and shots truly are inspired."

"It was your idea," Snow reminded her.

"In theory, but you brought it to life."

"I had a great time doing it. Sometimes, people want super boring shots, and I do it if that's what the client wants, but it's great when I can do something I feel truly passionate about."

"I can see your passion in your work."

"What about you? Do you enjoy your work?"

Amanda nodded. "I love it. I love most aspects of running a business, actually. The creative part is fun, but I also love advertising and dealing with customers. It gets my blood flowing, makes me feel alive."

"I wish I loved the business aspect. I actually hate that part of my job," Snow admitted. "Talking to clients is fine, but trying to advertise and sell myself is just the worst. That's part of the reason I joined the agency."

"Often the most talented people are the ones who hate the business aspect the most. I'm just lucky that I have a bit of talent in both areas."

"You have more than a bit. Look how well you've done for yourself!"

"In business, maybe, but not in my personal life. I'm fifty-two and what do I have to show for it?"

"Your personal life isn't a competition. As long as you're living your life as you wish—as long as you're happy—I don't see anything wrong with it."

"I'm not happy as I am, though. I miss Nicole—no, not Nicole exactly; I miss having someone."

"Do you think you'd get back together with her if you could?"

"No. Definitely not. Splitting up was a good decision. We were both just causing each other pain. I guess I'm just not used to being alone. I mean, I'm fine alone. Happy enough I guess, just sometimes it is lonely."

"I've never really been with anyone the way you have, at least not for as long. I've dated a little, but nothing ever seemed to work out."

"Is that how you had Bluebell? With someone you dated?"

"No, I only date women, it has always been women for me. I'm a lesbian. I knew I wanted to be a mom though. I used a donor to get pregnant and I was very lucky to get Bluebell. Do you date men too, or just women?"

"I guess I'm technically bisexual, or queer, or pansexual, something like that. I had a couple of relationships with men in my twenties, a long time ago, when I was figuring myself out, but I definitely prefer women. Particularly since Nicole- we had an incredible sexual connection. I'm not sure I can see myself dating men again now."

Snow wondered if she did it for Amanda the way Nicole did, but she was too shy to ask. "Did your parents accept you, growing up?"

Amanda's parents would be older than Snow's mom, which meant that they might have more difficulty accepting an LGBT daughter than Daisy had.

"My dad did, but my mom never did. They actually split up over it. I used to feel really guilty about that, but I've learned over the years that if they couldn't even agree on something so basic, they were never going to make it anyway."

"Probably not. I'm very lucky that my mom has always been pretty open minded."

"What about your dad?"

"He's never really been in the picture. He took off when my mom told him she was pregnant. I think he assumed she would get an abortion. I sometimes wish I had a chance to get to know him, but I guess it's probably for the best. He didn't sound like someone worth knowing, from what my mom described to me."

"I wish I never knew my mom," Amanda muttered. "She broke my heart when she refused to accept Nicole and me. It would have been easier never to have had her in my life."

"That's really hard."

Amanda sighed. "It was a long time ago. It's ancient history now."

Snow changed the subject to a lighter topic. "I know all about your business. What do you do for fun?"

"To be honest, not much. I use most of my free time to work. I technically have weekends off, but I end up getting bored and working anyway."

Snow couldn't help being a little jealous at that. "I mostly spend my weekends with Bluebell. I love spending time with her, but I sometimes wish I could have a bit of time just to myself. My mom can watch her sometimes, but as we live in the same house, I always end up involved with her care anyway."

"Why don't you get away sometime? Like a weekend trip?"

"Trips are expensive, and besides, I don't like to leave Bluebell for too long. She's used to having me around."

Amanda nodded. "You're a good mom, Snow. I'm sure Bluebell really appreciates you. I could tell how much she loved you when the two of you were at my house. What kinds of things does she like?"

Snow grinned. "She loves science. I never liked it in school, but Bluebell can't get enough of it. I swear she's going to be a great scientist and discover something awesome one day."

They chatted about Bluebell for a while more before somehow discussing what movies they liked. Snow loved romances, whereas Amanda was more into thrillers. They both loved to read mystery books, though.

Snow loved talking to Amanda. All vestiges of Amanda's original rudeness toward her were gone, which left her a pleasant and interesting lunch companion.

When they were both finished, Amanda picked up the bill, despite Snow's insistence that she could pay her half.

"Don't worry about it—this one's my treat. If you'd like, you can get the next one."

Snow nodded eagerly. She liked the idea that there would be a next one. "This was really nice."

"Yeah, it was," Amanda said fervently. "We should definitely do it again."

Did this mean they were dating now?

Snow didn't want to risk ruining things by asking, but she hoped so.

13

Amanda was already waiting at the door when Snow rang the bell. She opened it at once, beaming at Snow and Bluebell. "Welcome, please come in. Would you like some tea? Or hot chocolate, Bluebell?"

"Hot chocolate, please!"

"Some tea would be great, thank you." Snow smiled at Amanda as she took off her coat.

Amanda led them through to the kitchen and started the kettle. She was nervous, even though she had no reason to be.

She hadn't liked anyone in the way she liked Snow since Nicole. When they were together, everything was perfect, and when they were apart, Amanda dwelled fondly on the time they had spent together, as well as anticipating the next time they would meet.

She was beyond delighted that the Christmas cards had been selling as well as they were, not only because of the satisfaction of a successful business decision, but because it gave her an excuse to see Snow more often.

"So, have you thought about the kinds of shots you want to get?"

Ah, business talk. Now this was something that Amanda could do well. "Not really. I did buy some new Christmas decorations. I figured maybe we could use them somehow?"

"That would be great! I could get a few shots of the three of us decorating one of the trees?"

"That would be perfect. I haven't put up my tree in the living room yet, so perhaps we could do that one and hit two birds with one stone."

"Your living room does have great lighting," Snow agreed. "Then once the tree is done, we can get a few of Bluebell opening some of those wrapped empty boxes you have."

"No presents?" Bluebell asked from her hot chocolate.

"Amanda already gave you a present, remember?"

"I'll buy you another one, Bluebell," Amanda said in a fake whisper.

Snow rolled her eyes. "You're going to spoil her."

"Allow me my fun. I don't have any children of my own to spoil."

Snow's face softened. "Alright, but nothing too expensive."

"I make no promises."

Snow chuckled. "You're impossible."

"You like it."

Snow blushed slightly, taking a sip of her tea to cover her embarrassment.

Amanda wondered how Snow would react if she was bossy in bed. Nicole had never been into that, but Amanda had often wanted to try out a more dominant role sexually.

"Mom, can I play in the fake snow?"

Snow smiled down at Bluebell. "After the photo shoot, if it's okay with Amanda."

"Of course it is. We can make Snow angels, how about that?"

"Yay! I love snow angels."

Snow chuckled. "You know, snow angels would actually make some great pictures. Shall we do those first?"

"Yes, let's." Amanda finished her tea and stood up.

Snow stood too, holding her hand out for Bluebell's cup before putting it in the sink.

Amanda started up the snow machine while Snow set up her camera.

From then on, Snow was in control. Amanda didn't cede control to other people easily, but Snow knew what she was doing in this area way better than Amanda did. While Snow posed herself and Bluebell, Amanda fantasized about how she might take that control back in the bedroom.

They took photos of Bluebell making snow angels before going back inside and bringing out the Christmas decorations. Amanda hadn't been planning to put up a Christmas tree this year. It had always been something she'd done with Nicole, and she had thought that it would just make her sad.

This was the opposite of sad. Bluebell chattered happily as she put up various decorations and Snow clicked the camera shutter.

Bluebell posed beautifully. Amanda thought that if the scientist thing didn't work out for her, she could definitely be a model. Probably that is what happened when you grew up with a mom who loved taking photos all the time. When Snow took Amanda's arm to lead her into a position with better lighting, it sent pleasurable shivers down Amanda's spine.

Amanda wanted to kiss her, but she couldn't bring herself to regret having Bluebell here, even if it meant she didn't get to kiss Snow. She wasn't sure how Snow would feel about being kissed in front of her daughter, who would probably be confused by it, so it was best not to do so before discussing it with Snow.

The photoshoot took almost an hour, an hour that Amanda thoroughly enjoyed. When they were done, Snow promised to have the photos ready by the next day.

"You can take longer if you need to. I know you have other clients."

"It's okay. I'm looking forward to doing these. Besides, they're clean shots. I won't need to do much editing. I'll have plenty of time for my other stuff."

"Can you come again tomorrow afternoon? There has been so much interest in the cards that I want to do a number of different shots and take advantage of this while we can."

Snow beamed. "Of course! I actually have a few ideas. What do you think of having Bluebell pose as an angel under the tree? We can get her little wings and a halo. She's got a white dress that will be perfect for the shot."

"That sounds excellent! I'm going to the mall later today anyway, so I can get the wings and halo then. I was also thinking... what if we did one of the two of us kissing under some mistletoe?"

Snow blushed deeply. "I'd like that a lot. I think our audience would, too. I see our photos have been shared by a number of LGBT groups."

"I saw that as well. I love appealing to an LGBT audience, and this will do that perfectly."

"Tomorrow afternoon. I'll see you then, Amanda."

"See you, Snow."

THE NEXT THREE weeks went by quickly. Snow came over most days to take more photos, editing them that night and sending them the next day. She kept Amanda busy producing more Christmas cards, and even gave advice on the editing of some of them.

Amanda's favorite by far was the one of them kissing under the mistletoe. They had sent Bluebell to the kitchen with a hot chocolate for that photo. The kiss had been light but long, as they held it for Snow to take photos.

Once the photos were taken, Amanda had kissed Snow a bit more just because she could. The kiss had just started to get heated when they were interrupted by Bluebell asking for more milk in her hot chocolate.

Snow truly was a genius when it came to photos. She had endless ideas, and each one seemed to turn out better than the last. Amanda came to love being posed by Snow. As the season went on, Amanda needed to use her fake snow machine less, since real snow started falling.

Snow got some beautiful pictures of the snow-covered Christmas tree farm, but as idyllic as those were, they couldn't compete with the popularity of Amanda's family Christmas cards.

Amanda was practically raking in the profits for those. Snow was delighted by how well they were selling, and Amanda had to admit to herself that Snow's happiness over the matter was even more satisfying than the money.

Snow admitted that she'd never had much money, and she was suddenly in a position where she had way more than she usually did. She was putting most of it toward a college fund for Bluebell, but Amanda convinced her to buy a few nice things for herself too.

The shutter clicked as Snow took the photo, this one of Amanda and Bluebell laying out cookies and milk for Santa. Bluebell was becoming quite the star through the Christmas cards.

"Perfect. I think... I think we're done. Unless there's anything else you'd like taken?"

Amanda shook her head. "You've captured everything perfectly. We've done all the shots we thought up in that brainstorming session, and I don't think we'll need anything further for this season."

Next season, she fully intended to do another range of family cards, if Snow was willing. If she wasn't, Amanda would go back to doing her Christmas cards with just her trees. She didn't want to hire models to be on the family cards. It just wouldn't be the same without Snow.

"We should do something to celebrate." Amanda knew they had already celebrated the cards' success a few weeks ago, but finishing the last of the shoot felt like it needed another celebration. Besides, it would be an excuse to see Snow again sooner. Amanda would need to come up with more reasons now that they weren't seeing each other nearly every day for photos. It felt way too scary just to ask her out on an actual date without a business purpose. Amanda felt unsure of herself. She was so much older than Snow. What if Snow didn't feel the same way?

"Yeah, we totally should! What do you want to do?"

Amanda thought about it for a moment. "How about we go hiking."

"Hiking? I never pictured you to be the outdoor-adventure type."

"I'm not really, but I know you love nature, and I figure you can show me a few things." Amanda wanted to be part of Snow's interests. She didn't dislike the outdoors, she had just never really had a chance to explore it, other than her regular visits among her trees. That felt different, though, as it was all on her property. She had never really explored in the way Snow seemed to do.

"A hike would be perfect. I'll get my mom to watch Bluebell for the day, so that we can go to one of my favorite spots. It's a bit further out, but it'll be worth it."

"I'm not sure how far I can walk," Amanda warned. "Remember, I'm not used to hiking."

"Don't worry, it's not that far to walk. It's about an hour's drive away, but the actual spot is not that far from the parking lot."

That was a relief. Amanda knew she needed to get fitter, and maybe Snow could help her with that.

"How about tomorrow?" Snow suggested.

"Tomorrow is perfect. Shall I pick you up?"

"Actually, let me pick you up. It's a tricky spot to find, so it'll be better if I'm driving."

Amanda nodded. "Then I'll see you tomorrow, Snow."

After Snow left, Amanda went to the mall. There was an outdoorsy type store there, and she made a beeline for it. She didn't have anything close to proper hiking clothes.

The store attendant was delighted when he realized that she didn't seem to know what she was doing. He took the opportunity to pile her cart high with overpriced and probably unnecessary products.

Amanda didn't want to take the chance that she would be unprepared tomorrow, so she just bought everything he gave her. With how well the Christmas cards were selling, she didn't even feel guilty about the splurge.

When she got home, she was the proud owner of a hiking backpack, a special cooler water bottle, practical pants and tops, both long and short, a sports bra, a puffy thermal jacket, proper hiking shoes, hiking sunglasses (though she wasn't entirely sure how these different from normal sunglasses), a picnic basket and blanket, a portable camping chair with an attached sunshade, a rain poncho and emergency fold up blanket, and an emergency flare.

Amanda chuckled as she looked at her outrageous purchases. Yes, the sales attendant had been lucky to have her.

She had also stopped by the grocery store to get some picnic food to add to whatever Snow was bringing.

Amanda spent the rest of the day anticipating her hike with Snow. She took a while to fall asleep that night, as she kept thinking about the next day, wanting to make everything perfect. Snow deserved perfection and Amanda wanted to give it to her.

When Amanda woke the next day, she dressed carefully and got her gear together. At eight o'clock, Snow rang the doorbell. Amanda eagerly hurried to the door and pulled it open.

"Hey. Oh wow, I didn't know you had so much hiking gear."

"I didn't," Amanda admitted. "I went shopping."

"That was quite some shopping trip."

"Let's just say that the sales attendant was very pleased to meet me."

Snow chuckled. "I'm sure. Shall we go, then?"

"Yes, let's."

They chatted happily on the drive, the time passing quickly. Snow was a fascinating person. She was a free spirit whose creativity knew no bounds. She wasn't like anyone Amanda had ever met before.

Amanda eyed the scenery nervously as they got out of the car and picked up their bags. Now that she was here, she wasn't entirely sure that this was a good idea, but she wasn't going to back out now.

Snow seemed to read the worry off her face. "It's okay, it's not far. Thirty minutes tops, I promise. Then we can settle down and have our picnic."

Amanda felt slightly reassured. She could do 30 minutes walking, surely?

Snow set a slow pace that Amanda could easily keep up with. Sure enough, within half an hour, they were nestled in a beautiful meadow with their picnic stuff spread out around them. Snow had baked muffins and made mini quiches, both of which were utterly delicious. Amanda's store-bought food just didn't compare.

Once they were finished eating, Amanda sat with her back leaning against a tree. "Come here."

She spread her legs and opened her arms. Snow blushed a little but did as Amanda asked, coming to sit with her back pressed up against Amanda's chest. Amanda wrapped her arms around Snow. It felt so right, sitting like this. She wanted to stay forever.

They stayed there for hours, sometimes talking, sometimes lapsing into comfortable silence. Only when a chilly wind picked up did they decide to leave.

They packed up the picnic stuff, but Amanda paused before putting her backpack on. She put a hand on Snow's shoulder, turning her so that they were facing each other.

Amanda moved slowly, giving Snow time to pull away if she wanted to. Snow didn't pull away, and their lips met.

The kiss was light and tentative, but as it went on, Amanda grew bolder. She pressed her lips more firmly against Snow's and pushed her tongue into Snow's mouth. Snow opened for her, letting Amanda explore her mouth.

Snow tasted delicious, like the quiche and fruit juice they had had for lunch, and something vaguely minty that Amanda couldn't fathom the source of. Maybe a mouth wash. Either way, she loved it. Bolts of desire ran through her body. The rush of desire that had been building for so long.

Snow pressed her tongue into Amanda's mouth in return. They explored each other slowly at first, but with increasing ferocity as the kiss heated up. Amanda's heart pounded in her chest and she finally had to break away for air.

Panting, she looked into Snow's lust-darkened eyes. "Come home with me." She made it clear by her tone that she wasn't interested in tea or photos this time.

"Yes, please."

The drive home seemed longer than the drive there. Amanda longed to slip her hand between Snow's legs and watch her squirm, but she wasn't irresponsible enough to do that while they were driving.

When they finally got back to Amanda's house, Amanda led them straight through to the bedroom. The moment they were inside, she pressed Snow against a wall and kissed her roughly with the passion that had been growing in her for weeks.

Snow moaned and returned the kiss passionately, her hands gripping Amanda's waist.

"Undress," Amanda ordered.

Snow just kept kissing her, so Amanda took her shoulders and pulled her back a little. "I said, undress."

Snow blinked up at her, as though not sure whether to comply.

Amanda leaned close, whispering in Snow's ear. "I want to do filthy things to you, and those things are not going to happen with your clothes on. Now undress, or we end this right here and now."

Snow started undressing.

The sight went straight to Amanda's pussy. She could feel herself getting wet watching Snow follow her instructions. Nicole would never have let her get away with being so dominant, but Snow was different. She just seemed to comply. And from the flush across her face, it looked like Snow was enjoying it. Amanda realized she liked it—a lot. More than she had expected.

Snow was so beautiful naked. Long pale limbs, small breasts with perfect pale pink puffy nipples. Small round ass. Thick blonde pubic hair. She looked up at Amanda, shyly.

God, she's so sexy.

"Get on the bed, on your back."

Snow did as she was told.

Amanda advanced on her, grinning widely as she envisioned everything she wanted to do to Snow.

14

"Spread your legs."

Snow hesitated. She didn't want to be a pushover. She was sure that Amanda didn't like weak women. Perhaps she should resist following instructions like this? It felt strange, to give up control completely and let Amanda take charge. In the past, when Snow had been with people, there hadn't been this kind of power dynamic. They had been equal partners.

She shouldn't like this at all.

Then why was it so hot? Why did she desperately want to comply with Amanda's orders? Why was the very thought of Amanda taking control of her body completely the most seductive idea she could ever imagine?

She felt shy and a little awkward.

But she spread her legs obediently.

"Good girl."

Amanda started kissing Snow's thighs. She sucked and licked her way higher up, driving Snow crazy with desire. Amanda let her tongue slip into Snow's wetness, causing Snow to cry out and jerk into the touch.

Amanda didn't stay there long, licking up and down in long slow strokes before moving up to Snow's clit, which Snow certainly wasn't complaining about.

The first lick felt like a divine slice of heaven. Amanda's tongue on her was amazing, so much better than anything Snow had ever felt before.

Amanda licked her until Snow was right on the edge before pulling back.

"Amanda, please," Snow whined.

"Quiet. You take what I give you."

Fuck, that was hot.

Snow felt herself quivering in anticipation of what might be next. Amanda was driving her crazy.

Snow watched as Amanda reached into the drawer next to them and pulled out some lube. Snow didn't see how that would be necessary. She was already soaking wet.

Amanda squeezed some of the lube on her fingers regardless and returned to between Snow's legs. Instead of going for her pussy, Amanda went further back, brushing against the entrance to Snow's ass.

Snow felt herself jump.

"What are you doing?"

"Shh, just relax. You'll enjoy this, I promise. Do you trust me?"

Snow nodded, "Yes."

"Are you ok for me to try? If you really don't want to at any time, just say and I'll stop."

Snow figured now was as good a time as any to try something new. She took a deep breath and nodded her consent.

"Just relax," Amanda repeated. Snow had never done anything anal before, not really that it was a limit for her, but she had never found herself in the position she was now. And she couldn't seem to resist Amanda's bossy tone; it felt like *whatever* Amanda wanted to do to her, Snow wanted to let her. She did her best to relax as Amanda slowly teased her anus with a lubed finger before pressing it inside of her. It burned a little, but that went away once Amanda stilled her finger. It felt so different from anything she had felt before.

"Are you okay?"

Snow thought about this for a moment. "Yes."

It felt odd, but not entirely unpleasant. Then Amanda started to move her finger, slippery with lube. As the burn faded, Snow started to breathe harder. This felt *good*. She never would have expected it, but Amanda was right. She did enjoy this.

It felt so intimate, as though she was giving her body entirely over to Amanda.

Snow reached a hand down to finger her clit, but Amanda batted it away. "You take what I give you. nothing more."

Still, she took pity on Snow and replaced Snow's hand with her own.

Snow felt the intensity building inside of her.

The dual feeling of Amanda's fingers in her ass and on her clit battered Snow with relentless pleasure. She had been close to the edge anyway and it didn't take much more to tip her over.

She cried out as she came hard, convulsing on Amanda's fingers, squirting onto the bed beneath her. The feeling of her ass contracting around Amanda's finger drew out the orgasm until it was just a single wave of pleasure lasting an eternity.

When it finally ended, Snow went limp, panting.

Amanda withdrew her finger and wiped it on the bed covers.

"Move further down."

Snow did as Amanda asked without question.

"I'm going to sit on your face."

"Yes, please." Snow gasped. She was shocked at Amanda's confidence and yet at the same time, utterly seduced by it. *Whatever she wants, I want.*

Amanda wasted no time in getting herself positioned atop Snow. Snow watched Amanda's striking body as she knelt above her and looked down at her with those intense dark green eyes.

Snow could see how wet Amanda was and she felt her mouth involuntarily opening, desperate to taste Amanda.

Amanda lowered herself onto Snow's waiting mouth and Snow met her with her tongue that plunged into her, licking her with the hunger that had been building within her for so long now.

Snow reached up to touch Amanda's breasts as she worked Amanda's clit with her tongue.

Amanda easily took control, setting her own pace that had Snow struggling to keep up. The noises Amanda was making were already kindling desire in Snow's belly again, even though she'd just come.

"Harder, Snow," Amanda encouraged in a breathy voice. "I'm close... so close..."

Snow redoubled her efforts. Amanda stiffened and let out a long moan as she came, squirting all over Snow's face. It was so filthy hot that Snow moaned too, swallowing quickly and instinctively. She was surprised, but in a good way. Amanda was so much hotter than anyone she had ever been with. Amanda had just taken her own pleasure on Snow's face and Snow was left drenched in Amanda's desire. She smiled to herself as Amanda got off her and relaxed down onto the bed. This was the hottest thing that had ever happened to her.

She had never wanted to come this quickly after a previous orgasm before, but Amanda affected her in a way no other women ever had before.

"I want you," Snow murmured, nestling up to Amanda and starting to lick her breasts. Amanda pushed her away. "You'll have me again, but only when I say so."

That statement didn't do much to solve the throbbing problem between Snow's legs—if anything, it made her more turned on than ever.

She whimpered but didn't protest. She reached a hand down to her clit, watching Amanda to see if she would forbid it.

"You can touch yourself, but don't come."

Snow nodded eagerly. She rubbed on her clit as Amanda watched her intently, until her orgasm was mere seconds away. "Amanda, can I come, please?"

"No."

Snow moaned and jerked her hand away just in time to stave off her orgasm.

Amanda replaced Snow's hand with hers. "Don't come," she warned.

Snow panted heavily as Amanda rubbed on her clit. "Amanda, if you keep doing that, I'm going to come."

"Don't you dare come."

"I can't help it! Fuck, Amanda, I'm going to come! I'm going to come *right now!*"

Amanda pulled her hand away, but it was too late. Snow's entire body contracted, and her pussy gushed, but there was no pleasure.

It was a strange feeling. Releasing of tension without

the accompanying bliss. Snow didn't like it at all. Amanda had moved her hand off Snow's clit, and Snow quickly put her own fingers on herself, but her clit was now overly sensitized and didn't want to be touched.

She had known what a ruined orgasm was from the porn she had read, but she'd never experienced it before.

"Amanda," Snow whined. "Please."

"If you're good, I'll let you have a proper orgasm later. For now, come and cuddle with me."

Snow wasn't going to object to cuddles. They moved the blankets so that they weren't lying on any wet spots and lay in each other's arms. Snow pressed her back against Amanda's chest, sighing contentedly.

In this moment, she had no worries, no responsibilities, nothing but the bliss of being in Amanda's arms. Everything was perfect, and she never wanted it to end.

15

Amanda stared at her computer screen, but she wasn't really seeing it. She was too busy thinking about Snow. She had felt so alive with her yesterday, more alive than she'd felt since Nicole left —not to mention more turned on.

There was something about Snow's wide eyed obedient innocence in the bedroom that was more seductive than anything else Amanda could imagine.

She wanted to see Snow again. She knew that they needed to define what they were. Were they dating? Girlfriends? Maybe she could ask Snow to come over and discuss it then. Yes, that's what she should do. She wanted to ask Snow to be her girlfriend. Amanda grinned at the thought.

She sent Snow a quick text, asking if she wanted to come over for dinner. Snow responded almost immediately saying that she'd love to.

Amanda abandoned her pretense at work and grabbed her purse. She wanted to cook a nice dinner for

Snow. She'd make it a proper romantic dinner, with roses and candles and everything.

Amanda spent the next few hours preparing a challenging dish.

She was halfway through it when her phone started ringing. She snatched it up, thinking it might be Snow. She looked at the caller ID just in time.

What was Nicole doing calling her?

Amanda didn't answer. She had no desire to talk to Nicole, especially now, when she was preparing for a date with Snow.

Nicole left a voice message, which Amanda reluctantly opened.

"Amanda, we need to talk. It's about the divorce. Call me."

Amanda bristled at Nicole's tone. Nicole had no right to make demands of her. She had lost that right when she had left Amanda.

Amanda couldn't wait to get the divorce finalized. She already thought of herself as divorced, but she technically wasn't yet.

She wondered if she should have told Snow about that technicality before they'd had sex. Would it have made a difference to Snow?

No, probably not, Amanda decided. Snow was easy going, not at all like Nicole. She wouldn't mind. Amanda's heart was free, even if she wasn't completely disentangled from Nicole legally yet.

Amanda didn't call Nicole back. Whatever it was, Nicole would need to sort it out herself. Their lawyers were handling the divorce. If it was about the divorce, Nicole knew that she needed to have her lawyer contact Amanda's. Anything else Nicole might have to say to her wasn't important.

Amanda went back to cooking her chicken dish.

While it was in the oven, she laid out the table, turning the lights to dim and putting the red roses she'd bought in a vase on the table.

She had just finished getting dressed when Snow rang the doorbell. Amanda glanced down the length of Snow's body as she opened the door. She looked stunning in a pair of white leggings with a slightly darker snowflake pattern on them, and a dark blue top with white swirls that made it look like a snowstorm.

"Snow. Come in." Amanda couldn't help pressing a light kiss to Snow's lips. Snow leaned into the kiss, smiling into Amanda's mouth. They kissed for a few moments before Amanda broke away.

"I've got dinner in the oven."

"It smells delicious."

"I hope it tastes as good as it smells. It's more challenging than what I usually cook."

"I'm sure it'll be great."

To Amanda's surprise, Snow was right. The food was delicious. Amanda had a store-bought dessert—chocolate mousse cake with raspberries. It was even better than the chicken, and they both had seconds.

Despite the fact that they had seen each other the previous day, they didn't struggle for things to talk about. Snow told Amanda about the photoshoot she had done for a client earlier in the day, and Amanda updated her on the sales of their Christmas cards.

"You know, if you'd told me from the start that your Christmas cards would be outsold by Christmas cards featuring the two of us kissing, I would have told you that you were crazy."

Snow smiled softly. "I guess a lot has changed."

Amanda knew that she needed to discuss what they were with Snow, but Snow was so beautiful in this moment that she couldn't resist. She leaned over the table and kissed her.

Snow kissed back for a moment before moving her chair around so that they were sitting side by side. They kissed more deeply now, their hands roving over each other's torsos.

Amanda slipped a hand under Snow's shirt, wriggling beneath her bra to caress her breasts. She regretted not spending more time on Snow's breasts yesterday and was determined to make up for it today.

Snow gasped at the contact, reaching behind herself to unhook her bra, giving Amanda better access. Amanda took advantage of it at once, taking Snow's breasts firmly in hand and rubbing her fingers over the nipples.

Snow moaned at the touch, her sounds urging Amanda on. Amanda had to break away from their kiss to breathe. Snow's nipples were hard peaks in her hands. Amanda could feel herself getting wet already and longed for some pressure on her throbbing clit.

"Let's take this to the bedroom."

She took Snow by the hand and pulled her along.

"Undress and lie down on the bed on your stomach, legs apart."

Snow started undressing at once. Her previous resistance to Amanda's dominance was nowhere in evidence. Amanda knew that Snow was turned on by being bossed around in bed; she could already see Snow's inner thighs getting wet with her desire. Snow seemed to have realized this too, because she lay down as Amanda had instructed without complaint.

Amanda undressed as well and ran her hands over

Snow's delicious ass. She licked at the cheeks and squeezed them between her fingers. Amanda reached a hand between Snow's legs, rubbing the pucker of her ass for a few moments before moving further down.

She ran her hand through the slickness in Snow's pussy and brought that hand back up to Snow's ass, using the lubrication to press one finger inside. Taking Snow anally, especially as she hadn't had it like this before, really excited Amanda. Snow's nervousness seemed less than it had been the day before and after the first few seconds, Snow moaned and pushed back against Amanda's finger.

She likes it.

Amanda smiled to herself.

Snow was soon squirming as Amanda began to move her finger in and out of her slowly and deeply.

"I want you to come just like this," Amanda told her quietly. "I'm not going to touch your clit, and neither are you. You're going to come just from my finger in your ass, or you're not going to come at all."

"Amanda, I can't do it," Snow moaned. "I need...my clit...please, let me—"

"You need what I say you need, and I say that you're going to come like this."

Amanda felt Snow's frustration for a second before Snow quit her resistance and relaxed into enjoying the sensation.

"Good girl. I want you to feel every single part of this."

Amanda reached for some lube with her left hand and squeezed a little into the cleft of Snow's round ass enjoying watching it trickle down to where her finger was deep inside Snow.

She pulled her finger out and rubbed her fingers in

the lube up and down, teasing Snow's anus. She heard Snow's moans and watched as Snow raised her ass slightly, as though begging to be filled again.

Oh, this is so much fun.

Amanda pushed two lube coated fingers very slowly at Snow's anus and she felt it open for her and she slowly pushed deep inside. Snow's accompanying moan was very loud.

She pulled them equally as slowly out, and then back in, and then out, and in. Every time very slow. Every time as deep as they would go.

She felt Snow's body tingling around her fingers as though there was electricity passing between them both.

Amanda felt Snow's body opening up completely for her and she withdrew her fingers and added a third finger, also slippery with the lube.

It slipped easily inside and Amanda gave it a few seconds to allow Snow's body to adjust to them inside of her.

It didn't take long before she felt Snow pushing back onto her fingers.

Snow likes it. A lot.

Snow was rocking against her harder now, panting as the two of them worked up a rhythm.

Snow's noises were becoming increasingly desperate and Amanda could see the flush of red across her cheek as her face was pressed down into the pillow. Her blonde hair was a messy halo.

Fuck, she looks so beautiful.

Amanda knew that she just needed a little push to get over the edge.

"I'm going to give you ten seconds to come, Snow."

"But, Amanda—"

"Ten. Nine." Snow moaned but didn't protest, instead increasing her pace with which she moved her own ass as she chased her orgasm. "Eight. Seven. Six. Five. Four. Three. Two. One. Come for me, Snow. Come for me right now."

Snow screamed as she came hard, her ass clenching tightly around Amanda's fingers. Amanda grinned widely as she let Snow ride out her orgasm before she slowly and carefully withdrew her fingers. She hadn't been sure if that would work, but she was extremely pleased that it had. Her own body was thrumming with the need for release, but she didn't act on it yet, giving Snow a moment to recover.

Snow rolled over and smiled sweetly at Amanda. "That was incredible. I never thought I could come just like that. How did you know it was possible?"

"I didn't know for sure," Amanda admitted. "I just sensed that you seem to really like it when I boss you around and control you in the bedroom. So I thought maybe it might be possible. I've never done it to anyone before. But, my god, you did brilliantly. It felt amazing for me. You're incredible, Snow."

Snow blushed. "I do like it a lot when you control me sexually. And when you boss me around."

Snow sighed deeply. "I never knew this was what I was into, but oh my god, I am *so* into it. Would you like to sit on my face again?"

"Not this time. This time, you're going to do the work." Amanda lay on her back and spread her legs. "Go down on me, Snow."

Snow obeyed at once. It was easily apparent that she had some experience in this matter. She licked Amanda expertly, long strokes, short strokes, sucking on her clitoris, pushing her tongue inside of Amanda. Her enthusiasm and her hunger for Amanda was what did it for Amanda the most.

Amanda left Snow to it at first, but as desire and need curled in her belly, she couldn't help winding her hands into Snow's hair and guiding her head and pressing it to her.

Snow let herself be moved around, focusing solely on Amanda's clit. She licked and sucked every now and then before going back to licking. It didn't take long for Amanda to reach her release. Snow's tongue felt like it was sending tendrils of pleasure all through Amanda's body, emanating from her clit and going everywhere, from her head to her toes.

"Snow—harder... Yes, just like that! Just like that, Snow!"

Amanda bucked her hips upward as she came, pressing her clit even harder against Snow's tongue.

Her eyes squeezed shut as she shuddered through the orgasm, letting it take over her every thought.

When she came down, she saw that Snow had moved so that the two of them were level. "Come here."

Snow eagerly came into Amanda's arms, nestling into her. Amanda held Snow close, never wanting to let her go.

The two of them must have drifted off for a little, because the clock had jumped half an hour later when Amanda next opened her eyes.

She got quietly out of bed, leaving Snow sleeping there, and went through to the kitchen. Amanda started cleaning up the dishes from dinner as quietly as she could. Snow must be a light sleeper, because a few minutes later, she came up behind Amanda.

"Can I help?"

"That's alright. I'm almost done anyway."

Snow wrapped her arms around Amanda from behind. "Any chance I can convince you to come back to bed?" She thumbed Amanda's nipples, which were still bare as Amanda hadn't bothered to put clothes on.

Amanda moaned softly as her nipples hardened. "Keep that up and we're not going to make it to the bedroom."

Snow didn't stop, rubbing Amanda's nipples slowly and softly, driving Amanda wild with desire.

Amanda spun around and kissed Snow fiercely. Snow responded in kind, and Amanda started backing her out of the kitchen. They almost fell over the side of the couch, managing to right themselves just in time.

Snow had only thrown her shirt back on before coming out to find Amanda, and she hastily threw it off before lying back on the couch. Amanda hovered over her. Snow was already wet and Amanda pushed her legs aside, running her tongue through Snow's juices before coming up to her clit.

"Oh God, Amanda! Keep doing that. Please, please don't stop."

Amanda kept licking Snow's clit, wondering how quickly she could make her come.

"If you can come in one minute, I'll let you come. Otherwise, you don't get to at all."

Snow nodded frantically, rocking her hips to get a better angle.

Suddenly, there was a loud knock at the door, but Amanda ignored it. Who on earth was it at this time of night? Never mind, she wasn't about to answer it, she was too busy getting Snow off. Whoever it was would give up eventually. Probably sooner rather than later when they heard the noises Snow was making.

"Thirty seconds, Snow." Amanda gasped before going back to work. She pushed two fingers inside of Snow's desperate pussy to give Snow every chance of orgasm. Snow's hips ground onto her. She was so wet. She felt and tasted so good.

Snow moaned and thrust her hips up and down on Amanda's fingers. Snow's fingers tangled in Amanda's hair pulling her face in tighter. Amanda chuckled and allowed it. Judging by the noises Snow was making, she was going to manage Amanda's 1 minute challenge beautifully.

The front door suddenly opened.

Amanda jerked her head up, gasping in horror.

Nicole was storming into the room.

16

A t first, Snow didn't understand why Amanda had stopped. She was so close. Just another few more seconds and she would be coming. She whined and opened her eyes, looking up at Amanda.

Amanda was staring in horror at the door.

Snow squealed and closed her legs fast when she followed Amanda's gaze to find a woman about Amanda's age glaring down at them.

"Who the fuck are you!" she stared at Snow and demanded an answer.

Snow was all too aware that she was naked and scrambled for her clothes.

"Nicole, what are you doing here? Why do you even still have the key?" Amanda moved between Snow and this terrifying woman who had barged in on them.

"What am I doing here?" Nicole shrieked. "What is *she* doing here! You couldn't even wait for us to sign to the divorce papers before finding some young slut for a quick fuck!"

Snow flinched as she pulled her shirt on. She screwed her face up.

I'm not just some young slut for a quick fuck.

Amanda cares about me. Doesn't she?

She waited for Amanda to tell Nicole so, but Amanda didn't.

"Nicole, you'd better tell me why you're here, or I'll have to call the police."

"As if they could. I'm still your wife, remember? Now, if you want me to sign those divorce papers, you're going to sit down with me and discuss terms. You'd know all this if you'd been taking my calls or listening to my voice messages."

"You—you're not divorced yet?" Snow couldn't help but feel hurt. Amanda had referred to Nicole as her ex-wife multiple times. Apparently, each and every one of those times had been a lie.

Before Amanda could answer, Nicole turned her full rage on Snow. "Get out of here, you filthy little slut! You're young enough to be her daughter! How far you have fallen, Amanda. Now get out of here, slut."

Snow's eyes filled with tears. She looked to Amanda, waiting for Amanda to defend her, but Amanda said nothing. She was starting at Nicole with daggers in her eyes. All of her attention was focused on her ex-wife—no, her wife, Snow reminded herself—and she didn't seem to have any energy to spare for Snow.

Snow grabbed her things and ran out of the apartment, trying to hold back tears.

She managed to do so until she reached her car. Once there, Snow broke down completely. How could Amanda do this to her? Not only did she lie to Snow multiple times, but she hadn't said a single word to defend her when Nicole had been screaming at her, saying vicious and cruel things that were so untrue. Amanda should have jumped to correct Nicole, but she didn't.

Snow started the car. She wanted to get home as soon as possible.

She didn't remember much of the drive home. All she remembered was rushing to her room and slamming the door shut, ignoring Daisy's worried questions. She knew that her mother would take care of Bluebell when Snow so clearly needed her space.

Snow lay on her bed, sobbing. Things had been so good with Amanda. She had thought Amanda truly cared about her.

How wrong she had been. If Amanda had really cared, she would have told Snow the truth. Snow would have understood. Divorces were complicated, and sometimes, it took time to get the paperwork sorted. She wouldn't have held that against Amanda.

So why did Amanda lie? Snow couldn't think of a reason, which just made this even worse. Was Amanda the kind of person to lie for no reason, just because she could? If you'd asked her a few hours ago, Snow would have said absolutely not, but now, she wasn't sure.

Perhaps even worse was the fact that Amanda didn't stand up for her. She just stood by while Nicole screamed that Snow was a slut, without saying a word to defend her.

Things had been going so well between them. Snow should have known that it was too good to be true. No one found someone so perfect for them. Amanda didn't truly want her for anything more than sex. If that had been the case, she would have defended Snow to Nicole. She would have told her the truth about not being divorced yet.

Snow had never imagined that she would be used in this way. Casual sex wasn't something that she did.

Before, sex with Amanda had made her feel amazing, but now, the thought of it just made her feel dirty. She'd been such a fool. Of course, Amanda wouldn't really be interested in someone like Snow.

Amanda was successful, glamorous, assertive, and all the things that Snow wasn't. She was out of Snow's league, and Snow had been a fool ever to imagine otherwise.

Snow wept bitterly for what felt like hours. There was a timid knock on her door. "Mom? Is everything okay?"

Snow sighed and wiped her face before opening the door. She was all too aware that her face was red and puffy, but she couldn't do anything about that now.

She pulled open the door. "Hey, honey." Her voice sounded awful, and Bluebell's little eyes were alarmed as she wrapped her arms around Snow's waist.

"It'll be okay, Mom."

"I know it will, sweetheart. I'm just sad at the moment, but I'll feel better in time, I promise."

"What are you sad about?"

"Someone I trusted turned out not to be who I thought they were."

"Who?"

Snow didn't really want to get into the details with Bluebell, especially since Bluebell seemed to like Amanda so much. "It doesn't matter. She's not part of my life anymore. She can't hurt me again."

Bluebell seemed satisfied with this answer. "Do you want to borrow my stuffy bunny? He always makes me feel better when I'm feeling sad."

Snow couldn't help smiling. "I'd love to borrow your

stuffy bunny. Perhaps we can both play a game with him. How about that?"

"Yes, please. I'll go get him."

Snow lost herself in playing with Bluebell. She loved spending time with her daughter. Bluebell never failed to cheer her up when life got to be too much.

Snow's phone started ringing. She glanced at the screen to see that it was Amanda. She frowned as she turned the phone onto silent. She didn't want to hear anything Amanda had to say. She had fallen into Amanda's trap once before, but not again.

Amanda would no doubt try to lure her back into bed with sweet words and apologies, but Snow had never wanted a purely sexual relationship. She wanted someone she could come home to, someone who she could trust with her troubles and who could help her raise Bluebell.

Snow did her best to push Amanda to the back of her mind. She resolved to return any further money she received from the photo cards. She didn't want money that was only a ploy to get her into bed. It made her feel like a sex worker, and while Snow respected sex workers, that wasn't the direction she was going in with her career.

She continued her game with Bluebell, doing her best to forget all about Amanda.

17

"**S**now, wait!" Too late. Snow was gone. Amanda didn't even think Snow had heard her. She had only fully realized that Snow was gone as the door slammed. She'd been so focused on Nicole that she hadn't even seen Snow gathering her stuff, but looking around now, all of Snow's bags and picnic stuff were gone.

"What the hell, Nicole! Get out of my house! And leave your key here!"

"Not until we talk. Now that little slut is out of here—"

"Don't call her that!"

"Whatever. She's gone now, run away back to school, so the adults can talk."

Amanda fumed quietly. She didn't want to argue with Nicole. The sooner and more peacefully she got her ex-wife out of here, the better. Even though the papers weren't signed yet, Amanda already thought of Nicole as her ex. Their relationship had been over for a long time now.

"What do you want?" Amanda growled.

"I want half the value of the Christmas tree farm."

"What?" Amanda gasped. "You can't have that!"

"If you want me to sign the divorce papers, you'll have to give it to me."

"But the Christmas tree farm is my part of the business! You've invested no capital in it, you've never worked to maintain or sell the trees, nor have you received any profits from it. In what universe do you imagine that you have the right to half of it?"

"Read the fine print, Amanda. The terms of our marriage are that if we get divorced, we split our assets evenly, and no exceptions are made for the Christmas tree farm."

Nicole had always been better at contracts and fine print than Amanda. When they had signed those papers, Amanda had been deeply in love with Nicole and had never imagined that Nicole would ever betray her in such a way.

"You know what? Fine! You want the money? Half of the profits are yours. I'll have my lawyer draw up the paperwork."

"There you go again, thinking that you can solve every problem by throwing money at it. I don't want your money, Amanda!"

"Then what the hell do you want! You said you wanted half of the value of the Christmas tree farm."

"Exactly. I want you to sell it, and I want half of the profits from that sale."

"I'm not going to do that! This farm has been in my family for generations. It's part of my heritage."

Nicole shrugged. "Then you can buy out my half. The property agent I spoke to estimates the net worth is two million dollars. If you give me one, I will sell my half to you."

Amanda could only stare at Nicole in shock. She certainly didn't lack for money, but she was far from having a million dollars. "You can't be serious," she said weakly.

"I'm completely serious. If you want to take this to court, we can."

Amanda knew what the outcome of that would be. In cases of joint property disputes, the courts typically ruled that the property was sold and the profits from the sale split accordingly. She couldn't let that happen. She'd do anything not to lose her farm. It meant too much to her. It was more than just a source of income. It was her home, the one place where she could find peace when the world got to be too much.

"What's wrong, Nicole?" Amanda forced herself to soften her tone. "Are you in some kind of trouble? Do you need money? If so, I can help you. Just please, don't do this to me."

Nicole's face hardened. "I've made what I want very clear. You will either accede to my wishes, or I'll see you in court."

With that, Nicole stormed out, tossing the key over her shoulder as she left. Amanda locked the door behind her and then sank to the ground, her back pressed against the wood.

How could this happen? Everything had been going so perfectly, and Nicole just had to ruin it all.

Amanda didn't know how she was going to do what Nicole wanted. Her head sank into her hands as she tried to come up with a solution. Even if Amanda took out a loan, no bank would give her a million dollars. She had only taken out small loans before, at the very beginning of her business. She didn't have the kind of record she would need to take out a huge loan.

If she wanted to take out such a large loan, she would probably need to take out a few medium-sized ones first, to prove to the banks that she would keep her word and pay them back.

What the hell was she going to do?

Amanda forced herself up off the floor and went to her computer. She logged onto her bank account. She spent the next hour trying to wrangle the numbers into shape, but no matter which way she looked at it, she was screwed.

Maybe, if she had more time, she could get the money together, but Nicole had made it abundantly clear that she wasn't in a patient mood. Amanda suspected that if she didn't get back to Nicole in the next week or so, Nicole would bring this case to court.

She sat back in her chair, fighting tears. She wished Snow was here.

Snow!

Oh fuck, Amanda had forgotten all about her. Amanda vaguely remembered how Snow had scrambled to find her clothes and had run out crying after a barrage of abuse from Nicole, but she had been so involved with her own argument with Nicole that she'd barely paid any attention.

Snow must be feeling so betrayed. Not only had Amanda neglected to tell her that she and Nicole weren't technically divorced yet, but Amanda had stood by and let Nicole say vicious things about Snow without saying a word to defend her.

Amanda had always had tunnel vision whenever there was any kind of conflict. She always dealt with the immediate threat first before turning to the non-threatening issues.

In this case, it was a mistake. Snow wasn't the threat here, but she was more important than Amanda trying to sort out her finances to appease Nicole. Amanda cursed herself for not thinking of Snow sooner. Why did it have to take logic so long to filter back to her brain when she was upset? It wasn't fair. She'd never been good at prioritizing during fights, and now it was coming back to bite her.

Amanda dialed Snow's number and waited with bated breath.

Snow didn't answer.

Amanda left a message. "Snow, I'm so sorry. Please, call me. Give me a chance to explain."

She wanted to add something else about how much she cared for Snow and wanted her to be happy, but Amanda couldn't think of the right words, so she hung up.

She wondered how long it would be acceptable to wait before she called Snow again. Half an hour, perhaps?

Half an hour later, Snow still didn't answer. Amanda had to restrain herself from calling again. Snow was probably angry and needed her space. Pushing herself on Snow when she wanted to be alone wasn't going to help Amanda's case.

She spent the rest of the day miserably alternating between walking among the fir trees and staring hopelessly at her bank statements. The numbers just wouldn't work. Amanda was doing well, but she wasn't a millionaire.

Even worse than her uncooperative bank account was Snow's silence. Amanda knew that she had fucked up big time. She had as good as lied to Snow and failed to defend her. Amanda knew that Snow didn't do well with confrontations. She had been relying on Amanda to stand up for her against Nicole, and Amanda had failed.

She called Snow three more times, all of which had the same response as the others: nothing.

Amanda curled up in bed that night, shaking with tears of misery. She wished more than anything that she could go back to this afternoon and change everything. She would have defended Snow from Nicole's verbal insults, kicked her out, then taken Snow in her arms and told her just how sorry she was. Maybe things would have been different.

If only she could go back in time and do it all again.

18

Snow glared at her phone. Sixteen missed calls and seven voice messages? Who the hell did Amanda think she was? Just because she'd hired Snow before didn't mean Snow was at her beck and call. Besides, Snow seriously doubted it was work that Amanda was calling about.

The thought of Amanda was enough to make her want to throw her phone across the room. Snow wasn't usually given to such violent thoughts, but she was hurting so much right now. She just wanted it to stop. Bluebell could tell something was wrong. Snow assured her that she would be better in time, but she was starting to think it might be a long time.

It felt like a piece of her heart had been ripped out. Amanda had taken a chunk of Snow's heart with her when she callously threw her aside. What was Snow worth to her, really, if arguing with her ex-wife was more important than defending Snow?

Amanda persisted in calling her, but Snow hadn't so much as listened to one of the voice messages she sent.

She was sure that Amanda just wanted to get her into bed again and Snow wasn't going to stand for it. The very thought made her feel dirty.

Her phone started ringing again. Amanda. Again. Fuck.

Snow let it ring. A few moments later, she got a notification saying that she had a new voice message. She tried to fight her curiosity, but eventually it overwhelmed her. Snow opened the most recent voice message.

"Snow, it's me again. Please, please, just talk to me? Let me try to explain. Can I see you? Any time is fine, I'll drop everything. Just don't cut me out like this. I'll do anything. Please, I'm begging here. Let me make it up to you."

Snow almost dropped the phone in surprise. She didn't know what she'd been expecting, but it hadn't been that. She had thought Amanda would deny she'd done anything wrong and imply that Snow was being the unreasonable one.

She wondered if she was thinking too harshly of Amanda because of what had happened. Until yesterday, she had thought that Amanda was a wonderful, kind person. The Amanda she knew wouldn't hold her pride above her relationship with someone she cared for.

The Amanda she knew also wouldn't just let Snow rush out of the room without following her, trying to explain or trying to defend her.

Now, Snow didn't know what to think. Which Amanda was real? The one she had thought she'd known, or the one who had revealed herself during the fight?

She decided that people were revealed to be at their truest nature in times of stress. Sure, Amanda could be sweet and kind when she wanted to, but if she wasn't willing to show up for Snow in a difficult situation, then she wasn't the kind of person Snow wanted to be with anyway.

Snow deleted the voice message and all the others Amanda had sent without listening to them. She even went so far as blocking Amanda's number. She didn't want to hear anything else Amanda had to say.

Snow decided to go through her emails, which had been backing up over the past few days. She was busy responding to various requests when she got a new email —from Amanda.

Snow grimaced, debating deleting it without reading it, but it had attachments and she was curious.

She opened it.

Dear Snow,

I just thought I'd update you on how our Christmas cards are doing. I've attached some photos of the latest batches I've sent out to clients.

Could you come over to do some more photos for me? Please?

We need to talk. I know I fucked up, and I'll do anything for a second chance. I just want to try to explain. If you still hate me afterward, I promise I'll stop bugging you.

Yours sincerely,

Amanda

SNOW COULDN'T DENY the temptation she felt when reading the email. What if Amanda really could say something that would explain everything? Snow desperately wanted things to be okay with Amanda.

No. No, she wasn't going to be that stupid again. Amanda had taken her in once, and maybe it wasn't Snow's fault that she'd been fooled, but if she allowed it to happen a second time, that would certainly be on her.

She spent over an hour composing her response.

Amanda,

If you would like any more photos taken, please contact the agency and they can assign you another photographer. I won't be taking any more photos for you.

I would also like to end the deal we have where I receive half of the profits from the Christmas cards. I have instructed my bank not to take any more transfers from your account.

Please do not contact me again.

Snow

She clicked send before she had a chance to rethink it. The email was very short considering how long it had taken to write. She wiped tears off her face. No matter how hard she tried, she couldn't seem to stop crying.

She had truly thought that she'd had something special with Amanda. Having it ripped away from her before it even had time to flourish was devastating.

"Snow? Honey, can I talk to you?"

Snow sighed. She had known this was coming. Daisy had given Snow her space when she first came back from Amanda's, but she was worried, and Snow couldn't bring herself to turn her mother away.

"I suppose so."

"Tell me what happened, sweetheart. Was it something with Amanda? You were so excited to go on that picnic with her. What changed?"

Snow sighed, wondering if she wanted to tell Daisy everything. After a moment's thought, she decided that she did. Maybe it would help to talk about it.

"Everything was going so well, I really liked her. Like her. Oh god, I don't know."

Daisy smiled gently. "That's great, Snow."

"When I was at hers the other night and we were, well, you know— her ex-wife stormed in. Only it's not actually her ex-wife like Amanda told me. Nicole is still her wife. The divorce hasn't gone through yet. She never told me. She always referred to Nicole as her ex-wife. How could she have sex with me when she knew she was still married, and I didn't? What if I didn't want to have sex with a married woman? She had no right to keep it from me."

Daisy was frowning, but Snow was far from done. Now that she had started, she was on a roll.

"Then, Nicole started screaming at me. She called me a slut. She told me to get out. I got dressed, grabbed my things and left. Amanda never said a single word to defend me. Not one, even when Nicole was screaming at me."

Snow let out a small sob and fell forward into Daisy's waiting arms. "Why didn't she defend me? I thought she cared about me. Why would you lie to someone you care about?"

"Oh honey, I'm so sorry this happened to you. People are complicated. We can't always fathom their reasons for doing the things they do. Has Amanda tried to contact you since then?"

Snow snorted. "Only about thirty times. She's begging to see me and explain, but I'm not that gullible. She took me in once, but she won't do it again. I won't be used by her again. I don't just want to be used for sex. I want my own happy ever after with someone."

"I don't think that's what's going on here, Snow. From what you've told me so far, it sounds like Amanda really cares about you. She's certainly made a mess of this whole situation, but I think you should talk to her. At least hear her out. You like her a lot; I can tell. Don't close the door on this before you know for sure that you have to."

Snow couldn't believe what she was hearing. "How can you say that? She lied to me! She stood by and did nothing to defend me!"

"I know, and what she did was wrong, but don't be too hasty to end what sounds like a really good thing for both of you."

Snow folded her arms, fuming quietly. She wanted her mom to be on her side. Didn't Daisy think that Snow would love to believe there was still a chance for her and Amanda? She had to be smart about this, though, and guard her heart from any further damage.

"I don't want to be used again. She was obviously just using me for sex. Even if I do forgive her, we're clearly looking for different things. I want a relationship, not someone who just wants me in bed and won't stand up for me outside the bedroom."

"I'm not sure you're right about that, Snow, but I'll leave it up to you. I just hope that whatever you choose, it brings you happiness."

Happiness. It certainly didn't bring Snow happiness to stay away from Amanda, but she couldn't stand the thought of the heartbreak that could come with going back to her. A small part of her wondered whether it might not be worth hearing what Amanda had to say, but she pushed that thought aside.

She was better off without Amanda in her life. If she kept telling herself that for long enough, Snow would surely start to believe it.

19

Amanda wandered through the trees, looking for the perfect shot. She could usually come up with ideas for photos without any problem, but she just wasn't feeling inspired at the moment. Snow was her inspiration, and Snow was gone.

The Christmas cards were still selling like wildfire, and Amanda wanted to get a few more up on her website before Christmas. She wouldn't be able to do as good a job as Snow, but with the photography tips Snow had given her, she thought she could do alright.

Of course, Amanda could hire another photographer, but she shied away from the idea. Snow was her photographer. She didn't want anyone else.

Maybe if she could get a few perfect shots, she could sell enough cards to pay Nicole off.

Amanda laughed bitterly at the thought. No matter how many cards she sold, she wasn't going to make a million dollars with them. It was just wishful thinking. She wondered if Nicole would allow her to pay off her share of the farm in installments.

Even as Amanda had the thought, she knew it was a no-go. Nicole had made it clear that she wasn't interested in negotiating with Amanda. Amanda was sure that Nicole was doing this just to be petty, to get back at Amanda for not being a good wife.

There were any number of things Amanda could do to get back at her, but she refused to stoop to Nicole's level. She thought sadly of the days when they had been deeply in love and would have done anything for each other.

That thought inevitably led her to Snow. She missed Snow so badly that it hurt. Amanda hated herself for what she had done to Snow. She had betrayed her trust by lying to her and neglecting to defend her from Nicole's vicious tirade.

Snow still hadn't answered any of Amanda's calls or messages other than that email. The email had sounded so cold—not like Snow at all.

Amanda knew that this whole thing was a mess and it was entirely her fault. She just didn't know how to fix it, not when Snow wouldn't talk to her.

Amanda wondered what she would even say if Snow did agree to see her.

The truth about the divorce had just seemed so complicated. Amanda wanted to move on with her life, and she already saw Nicole as her ex-wife. It had just been so much easier to call her that rather than explain the messy truth.

Even if Snow forgave her for that, Amanda truly had no excuse for not defending her. Yes, she struggled to focus on anything except the direct threat during fights, but that was completely on her. She should have overcome that shortcoming for Snow, and she didn't.

Maybe it was better that Snow stayed away from her. Amanda didn't deserve someone like Snow.

She blinked back a few tears and sank down to the ground with her back against a particularly large fir tree.

Amanda pulled her phone out and dialed Emily's number. She needed to hear a friendly voice right now— the voice of someone who didn't hate her.

"Hey, Amanda."

"Emily."

"What's wrong?" Emily asked at once.

"It's Snow. I—I messed everything up. She's gone, Ems. She's gone, and she's not coming back."

"Where are you? I'm coming to you."

"I'm home, on the farm."

"Sit tight. I'll be there in twenty minutes with ice cream."

Amanda smiled at that. "Thanks, Ems. I'll see you soon."

Emily was true to her word. She rang the bell twenty minutes later, holding a shopping bag that contained three different flavors of ice cream.

Amanda bit back a sob as Emily pulled her into a hug. "It's alright, Amanda. We're going to work this out, okay?"

"There's nothing to work out," Amanda said in a choked voice. "Snow hates me now. She won't take my calls or answer any of my messages. It's over."

"Tell me what happened."

"Everything was going so well. We had finished our shoots and we were out celebrating. We had a picnic date, and it was wonderful. We came back and had sex. It felt so right, Ems. Like we were meant to be together."

With anyone else, Amanda wouldn't give details of her

sex life, but this was Emily. The two of them had always been completely open with each other, and she didn't feel self-conscious about revealing a few details.

"Then, oh god, it was a total disaster. We were having sex in the lounge when Nicole came in."

Emily winced. "She still has a key?"

"Apparently. I guess I never thought to ask for it back. I just assumed she wouldn't use it, now that we're separated. I suppose I assumed wrong."

"What did she want?"

"She started screaming at Snow. She called her a slut and told her to get out. I was so wrong-footed by her sudden appearance and so focused on trying to find out why she was screaming in my house that I didn't think to defend Snow, not until it was too late. Snow grabbed her stuff and ran out."

"Oh dear. I know you struggle to multi-task during fights, but I guess Snow doesn't know that. I'm sure if you explain it to her—"

"There's more. I never told her that Nicole and I aren't official divorced."

"What? Why not?"

"It just never felt like the right time. At first, I didn't know her well enough to discuss my private business with her, and by the time I felt like I did know her well enough, I felt like it was too late to enlighten her to the specifics of the contract status. I didn't think it would really matter. Nicole and I would be divorced for real soon enough."

"You should have told her ages ago."

"I know." Amanda let her head fall into her hands. "This is such a mess. It's all my fault. It's no wonder Snow won't speak to me. I'll probably never see her again."

"Have you tried to explain?"

"I've left her so many messages that she could prob-ably file for a restraining order if she wanted to. Her only response has been this email. Here." Amanda handed Emily her phone, who frowned as she read the email.

"Well, you're right about one thing, she certainly doesn't want to talk to you, at least not at the moment. I wouldn't lose hope, though. She's upset and hurting now, and for good reason. That doesn't mean she won't come around in time. The two of you had a good thing going. Chances are that Snow will remember that."

"You really think so? You think she'll talk to me?"

"I think there's a chance."

"Even if she does, I hardly have an excuse for my behavior. She'll probably go back to hating me right after talking to me."

"Don't think like that. Things may work out. You just have to give her some time."

"That's not even all of it. Nicole wants me to pay her half of the value of the farm. She says it's in the terms of the divorce that we split everything equally, and she's not wrong. I just never imagined when we were signing that contract that she'd ever be so petty. I think I'm going to have to sell it."

Emily's face was filled with sympathy and concern. "I'm so sorry, Amanda. Is there no way you can pay it to her in installments?"

"I thought of that, but I doubt she'll go for it. I'll try, of course, but it feels like she's doing all this just to cause trouble for me. I know I wasn't the best wife, but she wasn't either. I don't see why I need to be punished."

"Nicole did always have a nasty streak. She could be

lovely when she wanted to, but I was careful never to get on her bad side."

Amanda nodded dismally. "I always knew she had that side to her, but I never thought it would be turned against me."

They were silent for a few minutes, each lost in their own thoughts. Eventually, Emily broke the silence. "Come on, let's eat some ice cream. We can't do anything right now to solve your problems, but we can drown them in a shower of sugar and cream."

"Now that sounds like a good plan. What flavors do you have?"

"Chocolate, chocolate mint and chocolate peanut butter."

"Peanut butter, please."

"Coming right up."

Amanda got them both glasses of wine to go with their ice cream. It was a bit early in the day to be drinking, but Emily didn't comment on it, taking her glass without complaint.

By her third glass of wine and fourth bowl of ice cream, Amanda was feeling considerably more cheerful. She did her best not to think of Snow, instead focusing on trying to outdo Emily in trying to think of the word with the most vowels in it.

The two of them giggled as they came up with increasingly ridiculous words that certainly weren't in the scrabble dictionary. Amanda capped herself after her fourth glass of wine. She was definitely tipsy now, and she'd need to be sober by this afternoon. She had some people coming to pick up their Christmas tree for the season.

Amanda would stop messaging Snow, for now. It

wasn't doing any good, and was probably just making Snow even angrier.

That didn't mean she was giving up, though. She'd give Snow some time before renewing her attempts to make it up to her. Amanda would need to think of something better than just sending increasingly desperate messages. Something to show Snow that she truly cared...

20

Snow got out of the shower. It was the first time she'd showered in three days. It felt good to be clean, but she was now exhausted and just wanted to go back to bed, which she promptly did.

She knew she had to pull herself together and move on with her life, but she just couldn't seem to do it. Daisy had been taking good care of Bluebell, but Snow knew that Bluebell could tell something was wrong. She hated worrying her mom and her daughter, but she just couldn't seem to get Amanda out of her head.

Snow hadn't left the house in three weeks, ever since Amanda had let her run out of the house without defending her. Snow usually loved being outside, but her bed was so much comfier and warmer. She just wanted to sleep and hope that this had all been a bad dream.

Someone rang the doorbell, but Snow ignored it. Daisy would get it.

A minute later, Daisy knocked on her door. "There's someone to see you, Snow."

"Tell them I'm asleep."

"I think you should see her."

Snow sat up. Surely not... "Who is it?"

"She says her name is Emily. She's Amanda's friend."

Snow frowned. What would Emily be doing here? She had half-expected it to be Amanda, here to apologize in person. Snow didn't know whether she would be pleased or annoyed if it was Amanda. She desperately wanted to see Amanda again, even though she knew it was probably a bad idea.

Curiosity overcame her and Snow got out of bed. She didn't make an effort to fix her tangled hair as she walked to the door.

Emily smiled broadly at her when Snow opened the door, but she didn't quite manage to hide her surprise at Snow's appearance. Snow knew that she had deep bags under her eyes, despite how much she had been sleeping recently, and her hair was a tangled mess, though at least after her shower it was clean.

"Hi, Snow. Amanda asked me to come here. She has a surprise for you."

Snow's insides fluttered, but she did her best not to let any of that show on her face. "I'm not interested."

"Please, Snow? I promise it'll be worth your while. Amanda asked that you bring Bluebell with you. She'll have a good time."

Snow hesitated at that. She had been neglecting Bluebell recently. Bluebell deserved some kind of treat, and she loved Amanda. Maybe it wouldn't hurt for Snow to go along with this.

Over the past three weeks, she had had time to cool off a bit. She was still hurt and upset, but she wasn't totally opposed to hearing what Amanda had to say anymore.

Amanda hadn't contacted her in weeks. Snow had

assumed that Amanda had simply lost interest in her when she didn't respond to messages, but considering that Emily was standing on her doorstep, maybe Amanda hadn't given up after all.

"I—okay, I'll come. Just give me ten minutes to get dressed and get Bluebell ready."

"Perfect! I'll wait in the car."

Snow hurried to her bedroom and tried to do something with her hair. It wasn't cooperating at all, so she simply pulled it into a bun.

"Bluebell, get dressed! We're going out."

"Where are we going, Mom?"

"We're going to see Amanda."

Bluebell squealed in delight and rushed for her clothes. Snow put on a light dusting of makeup, trying to look like she hadn't just been lying in bed for three weeks. She was relatively pleased with the result. She quickly brushed her teeth and went to collect Bluebell.

Emily drove them to Amanda's house, listening to Bluebell chatter about Amanda. Snow was nervous, but she did her best not to show it.

When they arrived, Amanda was waiting at the door for them. "Snow. Thank you for coming."

She beamed at Snow, and Snow couldn't help smiling back. It felt like forever since she had seen Amanda.

"Hi," she said quietly.

"Will you take a walk with me through the trees?"

"Of course." It would do Snow some good to be outside. She took Bluebell's hand and followed Amanda. Emily got into her car and drove away, leaving the three of them alone.

"Have you got a Christmas tree yet?"

"No, not yet." Snow felt herself blushing. It was

Christmas Eve. She should have a Christmas tree by now. Bluebell always enjoyed decorating their tree for Christmas. She hadn't even been planning on getting one before tomorrow.

The joy of Christmas was gone for her this year. The last thing Snow wanted was to do something celebratory like putting up at Christmas tree when she felt so miserable.

"Let's find you one, then. It'll be my gift to you. What do you think, Bluebell? You want to pick out the perfect tree?"

"Ooh yes please, Amanda! Can I have any one I want?"

"Any one," Amanda promised. "Come on, let's take a look at what we have."

Bluebell rushed through the trees, looking at each one and talking excitedly about how pretty they all were. Eventually, she stopped by a beautiful, tall pine with thick needles and a couple of pinecones.

"This one!"

"Are you sure? It's a very important decision, you know." Amanda smiled down at Bluebell.

"Yes, I'm sure! This one."

"Very well." Amanda pulled out a notepad, wrote Snow's name on one of the sticky notes and stuck it to the trunk of the tree. "I'll have my guy cut it down and deliver it to you by tonight."

"Thanks, Amanda." It warmed Snow's heart to see how happy Bluebell was.

"Can we talk, Snow?"

Snow glanced at Bluebell, who was bouncing excitedly on the spot. "Yeah, I guess so. Shall we go inside?"

"Let's do that." Amanda led them inside and set Bluebell on the lounge floor with a couple of dolls that Snow suspected she had bought specially for this. They certainly looked new and unused.

Amanda and Snow went into the kitchen. "Do you want some tea?"

"Yes, please." It was cold outside and Snow could use some tea to warm up.

It felt a bit awkward. They were quiet as Amanda made the tea. Snow sat down opposite Amanda, her eyes on her mug.

Amanda took a deep breath. "Snow, I can't even begin to tell you how sorry I am. How I acted was wrong, and I'm not trying to make excuses, but I'd like to explain it to you, if I can."

Snow shrugged. She wasn't sure if she wanted to hear this, but it was too late to back out now.

"My parents argued a lot when I was younger. I was always the one to break up the arguments. I think that's why, whenever there's a fight going on, I find it very difficult to focus on anything except the subject of the fight. I should have defended you when Nicole said those awful things about you, but I didn't, and I'm so sorry for that. I had tunnel vision, and by the time I could see clearly again, you were gone."

Snow took a moment to digest this. She supposed it made sense. After all, Amanda had also been in shock when Nicole had stormed in. If this was something she had struggled with before, it was no wonder that she wasn't at her best in the moment. It still hurt that Amanda hadn't defended her, but at least Snow could understand it a little.

"You never told me you and Nicole weren't properly divorced yet." Snow couldn't keep the accusing note out of her voice.

"I know. I'm so sorry, Snow. I've been divorced emotionally from Nicole for a long time now. The practicalities don't matter so much to me, but I should have realized that they would matter to you. It just never felt like the right time to tell you, and I figured that Nicole and I would be properly divorced soon anyway, so it wouldn't make any difference."

Snow sighed. She wished what Amanda was saying didn't make sense, but it did.

"You hurt me, Amanda. I understand your reasons, but you still hurt me. You made me feel like nothing more than a sex object."

Amanda reached across the table, taking Snow's hands. "You're so much more than that, Snow. I love you. I'm in love with you, and I want to be with you more than anything. Please, give me another chance. Forgive me? I can't bear knowing that you hate me."

Snow's heart rose into her throat. Amanda was saying everything Snow needed to hear, and Snow's doubts were melting away like snow before a fire. She could practically feel her heart mending. Amanda loved her.

"I love you too, Amanda. I want to be with you. I could never hate you. Of course I forgive you."

Amanda came around the table and wrapped her arms tightly around Snow. "Thank you," she whispered. "You'll never regret it, I promise you."

Snow believed her.

The two of them went to the living room and nestled on the couch together, watching Bluebell play.

"What did Nicole want?" Snow asked.

"She wants half the value of the Christmas tree farm in the divorce. If I don't pay up, she'll take the matter to court. The farm will probably have to be sold."

"No!" Snow gasped. "Isn't there anything we can do? Is there anything I can do? I could try to help raise the money..."

Amanda pressed a kiss to Snow's temple. "It's okay, Snow. I was really freaked out at first, as I didn't know how I would come up with the money, but I have it sorted."

"You do?"

"I do. That's the other thing I wanted to give you— some good news, if you'll accept. You see, I've been approached by a big company that saw the photos you took of me. They want me to be in this commercial they're doing, and they're willing to pay handsomely. Added to what I've earned from the Christmas cards this season, it'll be enough to pay Nicole off."

"That's great!" Snow gripped Amanda's hands tightly in hers. She knew how much Amanda loved her Christmas tree farm and was more than relieved that Amanda had found a way out of selling it.

"There's more. I told them yes, but only if I could pick the photographer. I told them I want you, and they agreed."

Snow felt her mouth pop open. "But—but I've never shot a commercial before. Why would they agree to that?"

"I told them how brilliant you are and showed them some of the other photos you have taken. They agreed that if you're willing to do a quick course on video photography, which they will provide, they're happy for you to do the shoot."

Snow couldn't believe it. This was more than she had ever hoped for in her career. This was... It was just incredible.

She threw her arms around Amanda, hugging her tightly.

"Is that a yes?"

"Yes, of course it's a yes, you wonderful woman! I can't believe it..."

"You'd better believe it, because it'll be a reality in just a few weeks. I'll tell them today that you said yes."

"Come over tomorrow," Snow said impulsively. "For Christmas dinner with my mom, Bluebell and me."

Amanda beamed at her. "I'd love to." She leaned forward to kiss Snow, but hesitated, glancing at Bluebell.

"It's okay." Snow put a hand on Amanda's cheek, drawing Amanda's gaze back to her. "Bluebell understands that adults who love each other kiss sometimes. Don't you, honey?"

Bluebell made a face. "I still say it's gross."

"Look away, then, because I'm going to kiss Amanda now."

Bluebell turned back to her doll and Snow kissed Amanda gently. They kissed for several minutes, a slow exploration of each other's lips and mouths. If Bluebell wasn't here, the kiss probably would have turned heated, but as it was, they remained on a low simmer.

When they finally broke apart, they were both flushed and grinning widely.

Snow couldn't believe that just this morning, she had woken up feeling hopeless and unbearably sad. Now, she was so happy that she was sure she must be glowing from pure joy. With Amanda back in her life, everything was right with the world.

EPILOGUE

Three years later

CHRISTMAS WAS COLD THAT YEAR. Snow didn't mind. It just gave her an excuse to cuddle up closer to Amanda.

She yawned as she woke, pulling the blankets up higher around her chin, pressing her face into Amanda's shoulder.

Amanda stirred at the movement. "Good morning, Snow."

"Good morning, Amanda." Snow grinned and kissed her wife slowly, teasingly. Amanda's sleepy eyes became less sleepy as she returned the kiss.

"Merry Christmas," Snow murmured between kisses.

"The merriest," Amanda breathed back.

"You say that every year."

"That's because every year with you is better than the last."

Snow felt herself blushing. She kissed Amanda more deeply, moaning at the feeling of Amanda's tongue in her mouth.

"I love you," Snow mumbled into the kiss.

"I love you too." Amanda kissed Snow again, sending pleasurable shivers all through her body.

The door burst open. "Mom, gross! Stop it, I want to open presents!"

Snow chuckled as she pulled back. "Alright, Bluebell, I'm coming."

She and Amanda pulled on robes and followed Bluebell through to the Christmas tree, which had stacks of presents underneath it.

Snow had been worried about Bluebell at first, moving into Amanda's big house surrounded by the Christmas tree farm, but Bluebell had taken to it like a fish to water. She loved living here almost as much as Snow did. They still saw Daisy regularly, who was coming over later that morning.

"Just a couple gifts for now, kiddo. Your grandmother will be here soon," Snow said as she sat near the tree. Bluebell looked disappointed for the briefest moment before grabbing a few presents with her name on them and tearing into the first one.

"I still say you spoil her," Snow told Amanda as Bluebell unwrapped a new iPhone.

"She deserves it. You both do."

Their Christmas card business was booming, as it had been for the last three years. Amanda's frequent appearances in Christmas commercials helped to boost their sales.

Before Bluebell could open anything else, the doorbell

rang. Snow answered the door, letting Daisy in along with a flurry of snow.

"Where's my favorite girl?"

Bluebell shrieked in delight and flung herself into Daisy's arms. "Can we open the rest of the presents now?"

Daisy chuckled. "If it's okay with your moms."

Bluebell turned to Snow and Amanda. "Can we, please?"

"Of course, honey." Amanda kissed Bluebell on the forehead. "You go ahead and start opening."

The three adults sat on chairs while Bluebell handed them presents with their names on the wrapping before starting in on hers.

Bluebell exclaimed in delight over the microscope she'd gotten from Amanda and Snow.

Snow opened Amanda's gift, which was a beautifully carved silver snowflake necklace with what looked like a diamond in the middle.

"It's beautiful," she whispered.

"Just as beautiful as you. Here, let me help you put it on."

Snow leaned close as Amanda fastened the necklace behind her neck.

Amanda gasped as she opened Snow's gift. It was a photo album consisting of dozens of photos of the two of them that Snow had taken over the years. There were a number of photos that included Bluebell and Daisy too— the whole family.

Amanda leaned over and kissed Snow. "It's perfect; I love it."

"I'm glad."

Bluebell had finished opening her presents by now

and was fidgeting. "Can I go outside and play in the snow?"

"I can take her," Daisy volunteered.

"Go ahead." Snow was still staring into Amanda's eyes. "We're staying in."

Daisy chuckled and took Bluebell's hand.

As soon as they were out of the room, Snow stood up and held her hand out for Amanda. "Bedroom?"

"Bedroom," Amanda agreed eagerly.

Snow dashed through to the bedroom and managed to be undressed and lying across the bed in a seductive pose by the time Amanda walked in.

Amanda's eyes widened as she took in Snow. "I'll never get over how beautiful you are."

"Right back at you, gorgeous. Now come here and take your clothes off."

Amanda raised an eyebrow. "Someone is being awfully bossy."

Snow lowered her eyes in submission, her heart quickening with desire.

"Keep your eyes closed."

Snow did as Amanda asked, and she didn't regret it. Amanda's mouth was suddenly on her clit, and it felt so perfectly divine that Snow cried out, thankful that Bluebell was out of the house at the moment.

Amanda mouth worked on her while fiddling with something to their left. Snow had an idea of what it might be, and was proved right a moment later when Amanda slipped a lubed finger into her ass.

Snow moaned and rocked against Amanda's finger as Amanda kept licking her clit. The double stimulation was divine and quickly worked Snow up to the edge of release.

"Amanda, I'm going to come. Please, let me come, Amanda. Please."

"Well, it is Christmas. I think you deserve a Christmas orgasm. Come for me, Snow."

Amanda brought her mouth back to Snow's clit. That was all it took. Snow screamed as she came, bucking her hips forward, pressing her clit even tighter against Amanda's tongue.

Amanda licked her through it, wringing out every last drop of pleasure until Snow went limp beneath her. Amanda pulled slowly out of her. Snow whimpered slightly at the sudden feeling of emptiness, but she was quickly distracted.

Amanda took Snow's hand and brought it to her own clit. Snow started rubbing Amanda's clit with her thumb as her fingers worked their way inside of her. Amanda loved oral, but she also adored it when Snow got her off with nothing but her fingers. It was clear that this was what Amanda wanted now, so Snow set to work.

It didn't take long. Amanda started making those desperate little noises that she always did when she was close to coming.

Amanda cried out Snow's name as she came hard, and gushed on Snow's hand.

The two of them moved into each other's arms, nestling happily together. Snow could just see Bluebell and Daisy out of the window. Bluebell looked like she was making a snow angel.

"I love you," Snow murmured into Amanda's neck.

"I love you too, Snow."

Three years ago, Snow never would have guessed that she'd be here with Amanda, but she wouldn't have changed it for the world.

She loved her life with Amanda and Bluebell here on the Christmas tree farm.

Here, everything was perfect. As long as she had Amanda by her side, Snow knew that it always would be.

AFTERWORD

Hey! Thank you so much for reading my book. I am honestly so very grateful to you for your support. I really hope you enjoyed it.

If you enjoyed it, I would love you to join my VIP readers list and be the first to know about freebies, new releases, price drops and special free *hot* short stories featuring the characters from my books.

You can get a FREE copy of Her Boss by joining my VIP readers list : https://BookHip.com/MNVVPBP

Meg has had a crush on her hot older boss the whole time she has worked for her. Could it be that the fantasies aren't just in Meg's head? https://BookHip.com/MNVVPBP

ALSO BY EMILY HAYES

Have you checked out my Christmas Box set? Christmas Love Stories

Books included in this Box Set:

1: Coming Home To Holly- Jess is back in her home town for Christmas only to be faced with her straight best friend who she has always loved. *You'll love this Straight-to-Gay, Feel Good small town romance.*

2: She'll Be Home For Christmas- Lucy Beckett tries to hide her fame by interacting under a false profile online. But, when she starts to fall for the woman she has been chatting to, how will she find a way to reveal who she really is? *This is a warm celebrity romance that proves dreams do come true.*

3: Christmas With The Boss- Robyn has spent a long time trying to resist her attraction to her much younger assistant. She's doing well until they end up in a fake romance to fool Robyn's parents and one favor leads to another. *This is an Age Gap faux-romance with the Boss.*

4: Christmas Eve- Hardworking Nurse, Eve Foster, can't avoid her attraction to the beautiful medical receptionist. But the older woman is straight, isn't she? *This is an Age Gap Medical Romance that will keep you warm all Christmas.*

5: Her Christmas Love- Nightclub manager Mickey is useless at Romance. Her best friend helps her get a date on a dating app. Can Mickey fall in love for Christmas? *This is a hot butch-femme Christmas love story.*

6: Christmas in the Cabin- Nava and Dove have a friendship that includes sex. But Nava is adamant it will never become more than that. When they end up in a romantic cabin break, can Nava find a way to see what is right before her eyes? *This is a lovely warm Christmas romance with plenty of heat.*

Click Here to check it out! Read for FREE on Kindle Unlimited!

Printed in Great Britain
by Amazon